NAUGHTY HOUSEWIVES 4

ERNEST MORRIS

Good2Go Publishing

NAUGHTY HOUSEWIVES 4
Written by Ernest Morris
Cover design: Davida Baldwin
Typesetter: Mychea
ISBN: 9781943686438

Copyright ©2017 Good2Go Publishing
Published 2017 by Good2Go Publishing
7311 W. Glass Lane • Laveen, AZ 85339
www.good2gopublishing.com
https://twitter.com/good2gobooks
G2G@good2gopublishing.com
www.facebook.com/good2gopublishing
www.instagram.com/good2gopublishing

ACKNOWLEDGEMENTS

FIRST AND FOREMOST. I would like to once again give thanks to the man above for blessing me with the gift of writing. I couldn't have done this without you! The obstacles I faced trying to finish this novel are only the beginning to the ones ahead of me.

I would like to thank Leneek, Walid, Chubb, Merv, Demar, Rafeek, Du, Sheed, Knowledge, Omar, Dinky, Doe, Torey, Maurice, Yahnise, Symira, Amira, Nyia, Shannon, Denver, Danielle, Tara, Theresa, Burt, Meeka, Lena, Mabel, Lisa, Vanessa, Parrell, Shawna, Nikki, Rob, Gal, Terry, Ebony, Scoony, Ant, Mike, Rita, Tay, Kia, Grim, Brenda, Lyric, Jaimie, Zarina, Tanaya, Wannie, Megan, and everyone that I may have missed, love y'all.

To the people at Good2Go Publishing working night and day to put my books out for the readers, thank you so much. If it wasn't for your hard work and dedication, none of this would be possible. It is because of you that my books are buzzing in the streets the way they are.

I would like to thank my readers for continuously supporting me through this journey that I've invested so much time in. You made me who I am today, and I truly appreciate that.

To all my family and friends at the Cheesecake Factory, thank you for having my back and always believing in me. Arnold, Dom, Evani, Pam, Kayla, Stacks, Marcus, A.J., Jalisa, Shelly, John, Will, Mel, Rhonda, Ryan, Kyle, and everyone else holding it down out there, keep doing what you do. My new books called *The Factory* and *Supreme Justice* will be out in 2017, so look for them.

To my children, you're my inspiration to do what I do. I can't even explain how much I love you and always will.

To everyone else that I'm forgetting to mention, thanks for the support!!

PROLOGUE

AKIYLAH WAS HEADING BACK to the mall to pick up her sister. She had received a phone call and had left her there for a few to meet up with a friend. She didn't want her sister to see who she was meeting up with because she would get too suspicious, and she didn't need that. Vanessa was standing outside smoking a Dutch when she pulled up. Akiylah was pissed at her sister for standing out there doing that in public.

"Me told you about smoking that shit in public. You not home, Nessa!" she said to her sister as soon as she closed the car door. "You can get arrested here for that, or get a hefty fine."

She smiled, feeling the effects of the loud. Her mind was in a whole new place, and she wasn't trying to let Akiylah ruin her mood. She sucked her teeth and then rolled her eyes as she looked through her bags, not paying Akiylah any attention.

"Do you want some?" she asked, passing her the Dutch.

Without saying a word, Akiylah took the Dutch and puffed on it three times. Vanessa laughed at her as she synced her phone to the car's Bluetooth. She hit a couple of buttons, and Buju Banton blazed through the speakers.

"That's me song, girl, turn it up," Akiylah said, starting to feel the way her sister was feeling from the loud.

As they drove down I-76, traffic slowed down almost to a halt. This made Akiylah uncomfortable and impatient. She jumped on the right shoulder, weaving in and out of sitting traffic until she saw what was holding everyone up. She hit the brakes, but it was too late as she ran into the back of a disabled vehicle sitting on the side of the road.

"Oh my God, Akiylah, what have you done?" Vanessa said, panicking when she saw the passenger's head jerk forward.

Akiylah threw the car in park and hopped out, Vanessa following her. They walked over to check on the occupants. The lady that was sitting on the passenger side was holding her head in pain.

"Look over there!" Vanessa said, looking at the man lying on the ground in front of the vehicle, with blood coming from his mouth. She walked over to where the man was squirming around, and kneeled down beside him. "Are you okay, sir?"

By this time, there were a couple of bystanders standing around watching with their camera phones out, recording the scene. Akiylah didn't know what do because this was her first time ever getting into an accident. She called Sahmeer, but he didn't answer his phone. Vanessa helped the man to their car and jumped in the driver seat. Akiylah and the lady also got in, and they headed for the nearest emergency room.

By the time they reached the University of Pennsylvania, there were about five police officers waiting for them. Akiylah was scared straight and knew that they were there for her. When they parked, two officers along with a medical team rushed over with a gurney and placed the injured man onto it.

"Miss, we need to get a statement from both of you real quick," a female officer said, watching the man being rushed inside to surgery.

"She gave us a ride here! The person that hit him is still out there," the woman lied, trying to protect Akiylah and Vanessa.

They both looked at the lady in shock, wondering why she was taking up for them. Neither of them had the slightest idea of who she was. However, they were thankful for it.

"It's just procedure, ma'am, that's all. Can you describe what you saw, and how the front of your vehicle was wrecked?" the officer asked, pulling out her pad and pen to take notes.

The interrogation lasted about fifteen minutes. Then Akiylah was allowed to leave. The lady came outside to speak with them after she talked to the doctor.

"They said he suffered lacerations on his right leg and a mild concussion, but he will be able to leave today."

"Me so sorry for hitting your car and friend. Is there any way me can repay you?" Vanessa stated, feeling guilty about it.

"Actually, there is something you can do for me, and we can call it even. You won't even have to worry about the cops getting involved in any kind of way," the lady said, staring at Vanessa.

"Just name it, and me will do it," she replied.

"Well, can I speak with you in private for a minute?" the lady said, trying to hint to Vanessa to ditch her sister.

Vanessa picked up on the woman's vibe and gave Akiylah a look saying that she'd be right back. Akiylah nodded her head because she wasn't trying to get arrested for fleeing the scene of an accident. Her biggest fear was what her husband would think being that his family is in the spotlight. She didn't want to disappoint him, so whatever it took, she would do also.

"Me going to take a walk next door to get something to eat from McDonald's. Do you want me to bring you something?"

"No, me good, Sis! We are going back inside to check on her husband and talk. If you need me, call me phone. We won't be long cause we have to get home," Vanessa stated, following the lady inside the hospital while Akiylah walked over to the children's hospital to get some food.

Vanessa followed the lady into the restroom hoping that it wouldn't take long. She could tell what the woman wanted by the way she kept staring at her. Truth be told, Vanessa had wanted to taste her ever since she saw the way her ass looked in the skirt she had on. Even though she was only interested in men, she occasionally dabbled with the same sex.

"I've seen the way you were looking at me, and you have me wet right now. See?" the lady said, lifting up her skirt, letting Vanessa see the wet spot coming from her twat.

Vanessa licked her lips, walking toward the lady, who was backing up into one of the stalls. The door shut behind them, and they were all over each other. Vanessa dipped a finger inside her sopping wet pussy and then stuck it into her mouth. The lady let out a soft moan once she felt Vanessa stick it back inside.

"Get on your knees and eat my pussy," the lady said with authority, pushing Vanessa's head down.

She put her leg over Vanessa's shoulder and closed her eyes as she devoured her insides. Vanessa licked and sucked on her clitoris, and stuck a finger in her asshole, driving the lady crazy.

"Oh my fucking God, I'm about to cum all over your face."

No sooner than she had said it, her gushy load shot out like she had peed on herself. Vanessa sucked all the liquid up and continued eating the woman out.

When she came again, Vanessa began unbuttoning her pants.

"Wait, don't do that right now. I was just testing you out. Meet me at my house tonight and I'll explain everything," the lady said, passing Vanessa a card and then fixing her clothes and walking out with a smile on her face and feeling good.

***

When Kevin woke up, he tried to adjust his eyes to the darkness, but couldn't see anything. The last thing he remembered was sniffing some raw and un-cut dope and then everything going black. He didn't know it, but the dope had been laced with something. Kevin had moved on from snorting coke to snorting dope. Marcus told him that he needed to chill out from that stuff because it was affecting his game, but it wasn't that easy. Once the coke couldn't satisfy his urges anymore, that's when he switched. Now it was starting to become an addiction instead of a habit, and he knew it.

"So now you're on drugs, huh? Well let's see how you like what I have in store for you," someone said, startling him.

His eyes widened at the sound of the voice. Kevin thought he was hearing things, and started looking around trying to see who it was. When the lights came on and his eyes locked on the figure standing in front of him, he almost shit on himself.

"No, it can't be!" he said, looking into the person's eyes.

NAUGHTY HOUSEWIVES 4

ONE

"HOW ARE YOU, MY darling husband? I'm probably the last person you thought you would see," Michelle said with a wicked smile.

"You, you are dead! I saw them taking your body out of the house," he pointed out in disbelief.

"What you saw was them taking someone else's body out. If you really want to know what happened, I'll tell you," she smirked, pulling up a chair in front of Kevin.

He still couldn't believe that his wife was alive, and not only that, but also she was holding him hostage for some apparent reason. Kevin was hoping this was some crazy dream he would wake up from, but this wasn't going to be the case today. She lit a cigarette and then sat down in the chair. As she crossed her legs, Kevin could see the lace panties she was wearing. As uncomfortable as the situation was, he still found himself turned on. His wife was still beautiful, and she hadn't changed one bit.

"Why are you doing this, and why did you fake your death?" he questioned.

"There is so much to discuss, Kevin, but let me start off by saying, you made a promise to me when we got married, remember?" Kevin didn't say anything, so she continued, "You said that you wouldn't cheat on me and that should anything happen to me, you would take care of my mom. You lied about everything!"

"Michelle, what are you talking about? I've been taking care of you for over eighteen years and would have still been doing that if you wouldn't have faked your death," he said sarcastically.

"I asked you to place her in a home because of her condition, but you told Marcus that you couldn't wait until she died."

"I never said that! Your mom—"

"Stop lying, Kevin," Michelle shouted, interrupting his reply. He was appalled by her tone. "I saw it on the camera that was installed in the bedroom, so save those lies for someone else. Don't look so confused; they have been in there for years."

"You installed cameras in our home and didn't tell me?" Kevin asked, only to be answered with a slap across the face.

That told him everything he needed to know. She had seen all the countless affairs he had had in the bed they once shared, and the different number of groupies that had roamed freely throughout the house. He was busted red-handed, and there wasn't no talking his way out of this. He still wondered why she was doing this though! None of that explained the reason she had faked her own death or kidnapped him. He needed answers!

"You think I don't know about Sahmeer being your son, or that you were fucking my best friend the whole time you were fucking me? Well I know more than you think, and everyone will get what's coming to them," she said, cracking her knuckles.

"Listen, Michelle, I don't know what you think you're doing, but just untie me and we'll figure this all out."

Michelle gave him a deranged look and then stood up searching for something. She walked over and removed a pair of razor-sharp scissors from a toolbox that was sitting on the floor, and walked back over toward Kevin. Fear began to set in when he saw what was in her hand.

"Michelle, what are you about to do with those?" he asked, trying to break free from the rope, to no avail. It was thick and tied tightly enough that he couldn't get free but his blood could still flow freely through his body.

She didn't respond to the question! She reached over and began cutting his clothes off, starting with his shirt. After stripping him down to his boxers, she threw all his clothes into a trash bag. Kevin sat there anxiously waiting to see what was next. Michelle reached into her pocket and pulled out a cellphone, which Kevin soon realized belonged to him. She sent out a text to someone and then placed it into her pocket.

"Don't worry, my dear, no one will be looking for you for a while. You took a lil vacation because you were stressed out about everything."

"No one will believe that I just up and left without saying anything. Why are you holding me here anyway? What's your end game?" he said suspiciously, watching her every move.

"I'm going to get what belongs to me and then leave the United States."

"And what is that, Michelle?"

"Revenge!" she replied, reaching for his manhood.

She pulled it from his boxers and started massaging it. She just wanted to see if it was as good as she remembered. Kevin's whole demeanor changed as the feeling from her warm hand brought him to full erection. He couldn't help feeling this way despite his current situation. Once again, he was letting his dick cloud his better judgment.

"Oh God, that feels good," he moaned, closing his eyes.

Michelle knew she had him when he gripped the legs of the chair. She scooted down between his legs and took his erection into her mouth. The slurping and jerking were driving Kevin crazy as his balls swelled up anticipating an explosion. Michelle felt it also and suddenly stopped. She stood up and slowly unbuttoned her jeans. Kevin watched her as she slid them down, exposing the lace panties she had on.

"Do you miss this pussy?" she asked, pulling them to the side and then sticking two fingers inside her already wet mound.

The only thing Kevin could do was nod his head as he watched his wife finger fuck herself. He could hear the squishy noises coming from her pussy each time her fingers exited. Michelle teased him for a few more minutes before removing her panties. Her pussy was neatly trimmed and looked delicious.

"Let me taste you?" Kevin said, licking his lips.

Michelle sat on his lap, facing him, then smacked the bullshit out of him. He shook it off, waiting to see what she would do next. She lifted up a little, reaching between her legs for his manhood, guiding it toward her opening. Kevin let out a moan when he felt his penis enter her warm insides.

"How does it feel?" she whispered in his ear.

"Untie me, and I'll show you how it feels, baby," he replied, trying to manipulate her into releasing his hands from the ropes that were tied around them. He watched as she moved up and down on his shaft, enjoying each thrust.

Michelle rode him until she felt him bust inside her. She then reached down for something on the ground. When she came back up, she stuck a needle in Kevin's neck. He started shaking trying to break free, but she was still on top of him, and his dick was still inside going limp. She inserted the contents into his body, taking all the fight out of him.

"That's right, honey, go to sleep," she said, getting off of his lap.

"What did you just stick me with?" Kevin asked, feeling groggy.

Clearly surprised that the medicine hadn't kicked in yet, she pulled a little bottle from the box, and after filling the needle back up, she stuck it into him again. She only used a drop this time, not wanting to kill him before she completed her mission. His eyes rolled to the back of his head, and he went out like a light.

"Can you hear me?" she said, snapping her finger in his face.

When he didn't answer, she smiled knowing the medicine had finally run its course. She hurriedly got dressed and then headed out the door to take care of the next part of her plan. Before that though, she had to make a detour. There was a fire in her panties that needed to be put out, and she knew exactly who could do it.

Michelle parked in front of the building she was looking for and exited her vehicle. When she stepped into the elevator, she took her iPhone out and made a call.

"Are you home?" she asked as the person on the receiving end answered.

"Yes, what's up?"

"Open the door!"

The line went dead without a response. Michelle stepped off the elevator, heading in the direction of the cracked door. When she stepped inside the apartment, an aroma of steak and potatoes filled her nostrils, leading her in the direction of the kitchen.

"All this for me?" she asked, grabbing a biscuit out of the tray on the table and biting into it.

"Actually, I'm expecting some company. So if you don't mind me asking, what do you need?" her friend said in an irritated voice.

Michelle sat the bitten biscuit back on the tray and walked over toward her friend. She got so close that she could smell the scent of liquor on his breath. She reached for his dick, but he pushed her hand away. Michelle looked at him like he had lost his damn mind.

"I told you that until my business is finished here, whatever I want to do, you will do it or else." she replied, stepping back in his face.

"Come on, Michelle, I've been trying to get a date with this girl for a while. She finally agreed to have dinner with me. Can we do this another time please?"

Michelle wasn't trying to hear that shit. They had an arrangement, and he was going to abide by it. She started unbuttoning his shirt, but the sound of some-one tapping on the door caused her to stop.

"She here already? Aren't you going to answer it?" she said, sitting in the chair.

"Can you please just leave and come back tomorrow. I'll do whatever you want me to, without no complaining," he said with pleading eyes.

Even though Michelle had the upper hand in the matter, she decided to let him breathe this time. She stood up, grabbed her purse, and walked toward the door. When she opened it up, there was a beautiful woman standing there wearing a strapless dress and high heels.

"Thank you for your donation, sir. I'll email you with the receipt. Have a good evening, and it's nice to meet you . . . ?" Michelle said, holding her hand out to the woman still standing in the door.

"Oh, I'm sorry, how rude of me. I'm Stacy, and it is so nice to meet you," she replied, shaking Michelle's hand.

"The pleasure is all mine. Well, let me get out of here. I have some business to attend to before I head home."

"Give me a call in the morning," he told her.

Michelle turned around and gave him a weird look before walking toward the elevator. She had to admit to herself, whoever that girl was, she was beautiful.

***

Morgan sat in his office going over some paper-work with his board members. They only had two days to come up with a proposal that would decrease the state's financial problems. He wanted to save as many schools as possible, but in order to do so, he needed money. They were just about to break for lunch when Morgan's secretary walked in.

"Governor, you have an important phone call on line three. Would you like to take it now, or should I have them call back?"

"We are finishing up right now, so I will take it now, thank you," he told her, standing up. "That will be all for now, gentlemen. You have until the end of the week to present the new budget plans for the year, and I expect to have something on my desk by then."

"Are we meeting this afternoon or not?" the deputy governor asked, shaking everyone's hand as they began to exit the room.

"That won't be necessary unless you figured out something and have it ready to go by then," Morgan told him, knowing that he didn't.

"I'm going to head over to talk with the treasurer and make sure everything is in order. See you later!"

Morgan shook his deputy's hand and sat back down at the table. As soon as the last person exited and the door closed, he picked up the receiver and answered the call that had been holding.

"Hello, how can I help you?"

"We need to meet up today, and no is not an option," the caller said.

"What is it now? I have a lot going on right now and only have until the end of the week to get it done, so I won't be available until next week."

"I guess I will be coming to you then. I thought you said that I had the deputy commissioner job locked up? Why did I just get an email that they were assigning the job to someone else?"

"I have no idea of what you're talking about. No one mentioned anything about that to me. I thought you were doing a good enough job."

"Apparently not, because next month they're bringing in someone else. If that happens, I won't be the only one losing my job," Pete replied.

"Who are you threatening? I told you I didn't know anything about it," Morgan snapped, pounding his fist on the table so hard that he knocked the pitcher of water over on the floor.

"You're the fucking governor of Pennsylvania. Nothing gets by without you knowing. If you don't want that tape to resurface on every news channel and paper, you'll fix this, and fast."

Before Morgan could respond, the line went dead. His secretary heard the commotion and came in, with security right behind her, to make sure he was okay.

"Sir, is everything okay?" one of the big bulky men said.

"Get out of here, NOW," he shouted.

They quickly departed just as fast as they had arrived. Morgan's past was about to bite him in the ass if he didn't do something about it. He thought that Pete had destroyed all the evidence, but he should have known better than to trust a crooked cop. He opened his briefcase and pulled out a prepaid cell phone. He scrolled through it until he found the number he was looking for, and pressed the send button.

"I have an assignment for you. I will send you the details as soon as possible," Morgan said before pressing the end button.

Just like that, he had ordered a hit, but he had to figure out who would be losing their life. Would it be

Pete for his disrespect, or would it be the person or people that were trying to undermine his authority? His mind wasn't made up yet, but he would know something by tonight. He finished up what he was doing and then left the office to figure out what his next move would be.

TWO

THERE WERE SO MANY reporters and fans lined up outside of the practice facility to say their farewells to Kevin, but he had yet to arrive. It was his last day before he headed to Golden State to start his new role on the Warriors roster. Every fancy car that pulled up had the crowd anticipating an uproar, but it never happened.

"Where is he at?" the coach asked Marcus as they sat in the locker room.

"I've been calling his phone all morning, and it keeps going straight to voicemail. That's not like him!" Marcus said, checking his phone once again. This time he had a text message, and it was from Kevin: "Yo Marcus, I decided not to come in and left this morning. Tell everyone I said thanks and good-bye. I will see you around. Kevin!!!"

"Take a look at this, coach, it's from Kevin," Marcus stated, handing him the phone.

After reading the message, the coach left to hold the long-awaited press conference. Marcus sent Kevin another text and then waited a few minutes before heading home. As he drove down the highway, he wondered to himself if the maternity issue had anything to do with it. Kevin was not only his friend, but he was also family, and they were supposed to get through their problems together. They played each other in two weeks in Philly, so he would eventually get the chance to talk to Kevin if they didn't speak before then. He pulled into the gas station to get gas, when he noticed a familiar face at one of the pumps.

"You need some help with that?" he said, watching her struggle with the gas cap.

The woman looked up to see who was interrupting her, and smiled when she realized who it was. She hadn't saw Marcus since they graduated from high school, and here he was standing before her, looking very attractive.

"How have you been, Marcus? It's been a while," she said, giving him a hug.

"I know, the last time I saw you, you were cheering for us as we beat the shit out of Gratz in high school. I used to have the biggest crush on you. What have you been doing with yourself lately?" he asked, removing the fuel cap and pumping her gas.

"Well, I have been working hard while raising my twins on my own," Megan stated, giving him a seductive smile.

"What kind of work are you doing now? I saw your sister a couple of years ago, and she said that you were some kind of marketing executive."

"I'm still doing that, but now I'm my own boss. I watched you and Kevin's games all the time, Mr. NBA Star. How is he doing anyway? The last time I saw him, y'all were messing with those two gold-digging skinks."

"He's doing okay, and we married those two skinks!" he smiled before continuing. "Anyway, Kevin was traded to Golden State, and now we are no longer teammates. So where are you on your way to?" he asked, changing the subject.

"Oh shit, I'm sorry to hear that! I have to stop at the market and then head home to fix dinner for the twins. Take my number, and if you ever want to hang out, give me a call," she replied, storing her number in his phone. She had to admit, he looked way better than he did when they were kids. "I will definitely do that, and you do the same," he told her, giving her another hug and then walking over to his car to pump his own gas.

He waved to her as she pulled out of the gas station, wondering what it would feel like to eat her pussy. Megan had her own intentions of getting close to him, but that would be her own little secret. She planned on calling him this weekend when her daughters headed back to college. That way they could have some alone time and she could reel him in.

Marcus headed home hoping to get some rest before Sasha, Akiylah, and Vanessa returned from the spa. She told him that she was taking the girls out for a day of pampering. He wanted his family to go back to normal, and hopefully it would.

"Hey, Marcus!" Vanessa said, greeting him as he walked through the door.

"What are you doing home? I thought you were out with Sasha at the spa getting pampered as usual," he replied, sitting his gym bag down and looking in the refrigerator for something to drink.

"We did go, but when we were done I wanted to come home. They went to the movies, and Sasha said she would bring dinner home with her, so don't order anything."

"Oh, okay. Well I'm going to take a quick shower. If they come back before then, tell her to make me a plate and put it in the microwave," Marcus said, heading upstairs.

"Okay!"

Vanessa had on some shorts and a wifebeater, making it hard for him not to stare at her perky breasts. He shook his head at the thought of what he would have done to her if he had stayed down there any longer. He sat his phone on the dresser, stripped out of his clothes, and then hopped in the shower. The water was very soothing to his skin as he washed the sweat from practice off of his body.

After putting on some clean sweats, he looked at the number that he got from his high school crush and wondered if he should call or not. Finally, not overthinking it any longer, he pressed the call button. Someone answered after three rings.

"Hello!"

"Hello, is this Megan?" he asked, sitting at the foot of the bed.

"No, this is her daughter. Hold on, I'll get her. Mom, someone wants you on the phone," she screamed out.

A few seconds later he heard Megan's voice asking who it was. Megan's daughter passed her the phone, and she spoke through the receiver.

"Hello, who am I speaking to?"

"Hey, Megan, this is Marcus. Were you busy?" he asked, calm and collect.

"Actually, I was just finishing up with dinner. What's up, you miss me already?" she cooed.

"You can say that! I was wondering what you were doing tonight?"

"I have to make a run, but would you like to come over afterward? We can get a drink and catch up on old times."

"That sounds good! What's your address, and what time should I be there?" he asked excitedly.

"I'm texting it to you right now. You can meet me here around ten o'clock. You sure your wife is okay with it?" she said smiling.

"She will be too busy to care about what I'm doing. Should I bring anything with me?"

"No, just yourself! Talk to you later," Megan said, ending the call.

Marcus checked the time on his watch and realized that he still had about two hours before he had to meet her. He decided to watch the new TV series on Fox called *Star*. It didn't come on until nine, so he settled for *Lethal Weapon*. He could hear Sasha and Akiylah talking downstairs and decided to join them for dinner.

They all sat and ate the food Sasha had picked up from Buffalo Hot Wings. Afterward he made up some lame excuse to get out of the house, and believe it or not, it worked. He jumped in his Range, entered Megan's address in his navigation system, and headed for her crib. He made one stop, and that was to pick up a box of Magnums.

***

Marcus parked in Megan's driveway and saw that her car wasn't there. He thought that she had parked in the garage, so he got out and rang the doorbell.

The door opened, and one of her daughters was standing there. She was the spitting image of her mother. Knowing exactly who it was, she stood there with her mouth wide open. She didn't know what to say or do!

"Is your mom home?" Marcus asked, snapping her out of her trance.

"Uh, uh no, but she called and said that she would be running late and for you to wait here until she comes. You can come in," she said, moving to the side.

At first Marcus didn't want to, but when he saw her twin sister sitting on the couch talking to another girl, he said fuck it.

"Thank you," he said, stepping inside.

"Can I get you something to drink, Mr. Marcus?" the other one asked.

"No thanks! Let me give her a call to see how long she's gonna be," Marcus said, pulling out his phone. Megan answered on the first ring.

"Hey, you! Sorry that I'm not there yet. This client wants to go over all the paperwork for the new billboards that will be going up in a week. I'm not sure how much longer it will be, but I will text you when I'm on my way."

"So you want me to wait here for you?" he asked.

"Yes, if that's not a problem, and you can keep an eye on my girls for me. No friends over except their best friend, who should be there already, and don't let them get drunk," Megan replied.

"Your daughters are grown women, I don't need to babysit them, but I will make sure they don't get in trouble. It's the least I can do."

He disconnected the call and walked into the living room where the girls were sitting. Marcus noticed that they were all extremely beautiful. He sat on the couch across from them and studied each of their features.

Lacey was five foot eight, 110 pounds, with bleached blond hair, emerald green eyes, and 34C breasts. She had on a snug sweater that really enhanced them and a skirt with knee-high boots.

Gracey was five foot eight, 105 pounds, with platinum blonde hair, and blue eyes, which was the only way you could tell them apart. She had 34B breasts and a tongue ring that had her birthstone in it.

Gracey had on a silk top that showcased her hard nipples, and was also wearing a short skirt.

Their friend was also dressed to impress. At foot six, Jade had jet black hair, dark brown eyes, 32C breasts, and an hourglass waist. She had on a low-cut sweater that exposed her Victoria's Secret red lace bra.

"My feet are killing me in these," Jade said, bending over to take off her boots.

Marcus could see her dark nipples with rings around them the size of half dollars. She looked up and gave him a sexy smile. He knew she saw him looking down her sweater.

"Why y'all all dressed up? Am I holding you up from going out?" he asked them.

"No, we were supposed to hang with our boy-friends tonight, but they went to some basketball game with their teammates," answered Lacey.

"Well, I'm not waiting around for him. I'm going out with this guy I met at the mall the other day. I will see you when I get back," bragged Gracey, heading for the door.

"Have fun, whore," Lacey yelled out to her sister as the door shut.

"How old are you ladies?" Marcus asked.

"Twenty!" they both replied in unison.

Jade offered him a drink once again, but he refused. She moved closer to him, rubbing his shoulders from behind, while Lacey sat in the chair across from him and started to take off her boots also. Marcus didn't realize he was staring up her skirt, right at the pink panties she was wearing, until he heard someone say something.

"My bra match them too."

Both women burst out laughing, causing him to shake his head. He also had to smile at the comment. He apologized for his actions.

"No problem!" Lacey said with a smile, letting him know that it was okay. "I don't mind, I'm not shy about my body."

She sat with her legs slightly apart so he could continue to stare at them. Jade poured another drink and downed it. Marcus got up and went to use the bathroom. He told himself that he needed a break. He splashed his face with cold water, then let it run over his wrist. When he felt brave enough to return to the living room, he noticed that he could now see Jade's red thong sticking out of the tights she was wearing, as she bent over like she was doing yoga. His dick quickly rose to attention at the sight. When he sat back down on the couch, Lacey put her hand on his leg close to his engorged cock.

"Since we all have been stood up tonight, how about we enjoy each other?" Lacey said, rubbing his leg harder. "I've always wanted to fuck an NBA star."

Marcus was speechless. He had fucked plenty of groupies in his life, but there was something about them that had him very intrigued.

"Would you like that?" Jade said, leaning forward until her lips were next to his.

He nodded, and she kissed his lips. Lacey's hands moved slowly up his thighs until they rested on his erection. She then leaned in and started kissing Jade passionately. They continued to kiss, reaching over Marcus. Jade eased her legs apart and started rubbing her pussy over her panties. Marcus had let this go too far as he thought about Megan coming home and catching him.

He was no longer in control or able to stop it though. His dick was at full erection and ready for some action. Together, Jade and Lacey pulled Marcus's shirt up over his head and then started to undo his belt. As they pulled his jeans and boxers off, Lacey nibbled on his chest. She paused momentarily to admire his brick-hard abs.

"Your body has me so wet," she whispered while resuming her tongue action on his nipples.

"I'm trying to figure out why I'm the only one sitting here naked," Marcus asked, rubbing Jade's ass.

They both stood up and began to undress slowly. Lacey turned her back to Marcus and lowered her skirt and panties, with her ass only inches from his face. She pushed it in his face, and he started slowly licking it. His tongue ended up making his way to her pussy.

"You are so nasty licking my asshole. Let me see you do that to Jade," Lacey said, moving out of the way so Jade could get in position.

Marcus didn't hesitate as he gripped her ass and sucked on her insides like a vacuum. He took his time exploring both of the girls' bodies, and they did the same to him. After about thirty minutes of foreplay, Jade needed to be filled up. She stood over the top of him, positioning her glistening pussy lips over his body. She rubbed her pussy against his penis, coating it with her juices. Lacey got in between them and started stroking his erection while teasing Jade's pussy lips at the same time.

"Okay, Lacey, put that big dick in my pussy," Jade said, tired of waiting.

With that said, Lacey guided his dick deep into Jade's warm hole. She sat up and took it all the way in, then bounced a little to get deeper penetration. Marcus couldn't believe how tight is was. Lacey moved over and slowly lowered her pussy, which was completely shaved, to Marcus's face. Her clit looked delicious, and the fragrance coming from her pussy only boosted his arousal as her juices dripped over his nose and into his mouth.

He reached up and grabbed her legs, pulling her tightly against his face. His tongue made circles around her clitoris, and her body started convulsing.

"I'm cumming," Lacey screamed out in pleasure.

Jade continued to bounce up and down on his dick. He was so hard that it was hurting him a little. He continued to lick away at Lacey's pussy despite her trying to break free. He was teaching them a lesson about trying to fuck a baller. He was giving them what they wanted!

"Oh God, I'm about to bust," Marcus moaned pumping harder, trying to rip through Jade's stomach.

Jade just kept her hips moving, matching him thrust for thrust. No longer able to hold it in, he shot his load inside her. It felt so good to him that he didn't care about the consequences of not pulling out. Her muscles milked his dick, squeezing and pulling. Seconds later she also busted all over his half-limped dick. She eased off of him and started kissing him.

"My turn," Lacey said, kneeling over him.

"I'm not hard yet," Marcus replied.

"I'll take care of that," Jade said, twirling her tongue ring over the head of his penis.

Marcus's dick rose to the occasion in a matter of seconds. Lacey bent over in the doggy style position as Marcus entered her from behind. Her pussy was even hotter than Jade's was. His dick stretched her walls as he pumped in and out like a NASCAR driver. Jade squeezed her tits together as she watched the action, then stood over Marcus allowing him to now taste her panini. Her pussy was salty and musty.

He could also taste his own cum coming from it. He sucked at her pussy and took all his cum back. Marcus saw Jade's pussy muscles contract and squeeze a glob of semen out. It landed on his tongue and rolled down his throat. He reached up and grabbed her legs, pressing his tongue deep into her pussy and bringing her to another orgasm.

Lacey continued to pump back and forward, building to her own orgasm. As she started to convulse, Jade stuck a finger in her ass. That caused her to have an even more powerful orgasm. She leaned back as she came, and fluids dripped down his shaft, into his pubic hairs. Lacey wiggled her ass, releasing more fluid.

Jade started licking the cum from Lacey's pussy, causing Marcus's balls to tighten up from excitement. He pulled out, and both women swallowed his load as it erupted from his body.

"Ahhhhhhhh," he moaned with his eyes closed.

The three of them sat there for a few minutes, and then Marcus stood up and put his clothes back on. The girls watched him without saying a word. He had to get up out of there before Megan came home. He couldn't believe he just had fucked his high school sweetheart's daughter and friend. He had stooped to an all-time low, but he didn't regret it at all.

"Your mom can never find out about this," he said, grabbing his phone off the floor.

"Your secret is safe with us," smiled Lacey, giving Jade a kiss and sticking two fingers in her pussy.

As tempting as it was to watch them, he had to leave. When he got in his car and pulled off, he busted out laughing and knew he was going to see one of them again.

THREE

"**GOOD LUCK AT THE** meeting today, baby. I hope you get what you've been waiting for."

"Thank you! Don't make any plans tonight because we are going out to celebrate. This is going to place us right where we need to be, financially as well as politically," he replied, giving his fiancé a kiss.

He was on his way to get promoted from captain to deputy commissioner. Even though the position was promised to Detective Pete Davis, Captain Montgomery had more qualifications and was a decorated officer on numerous occasions. Not to mention that he outranked the detective in every category possible.

Captain Montgomery hit the alarm and then placed his suit jacket and briefcase in the backseat of his SUV. Usually he had a driver, but today he wanted to drive himself to 8th & Race to meet with the commissioner and the mayor of Philadelphia. He sat in the driver seat and shut the door. Just as he was about to press the start button, his cell phone rang.

"Hello!"

"You should have just left it alone," the caller said and then hung up.

Captain Montgomery's years of experience on the force kicked in, and he reached for the handle, trying to get out of the vehicle, but it was too late. The SUV exploded with such a force that it put a hole through the front of his house. It wouldn't have mattered if he would have escaped the car, he still would have died.

His fiancé came running out the back door screaming and shouting for someone to help him, but no one would dare approach the blazing furnace. You could hear the sirens approaching the scene from a distance. Onlookers were now filling the streets watching the tragedy that had stunned this gated community.

"Somebody please help him! Please get him out!" she sobbed, kneeling on the ground.

"It's too late, he's gone," one of her neighbors said, consoling her as they watched his corpse burn to a crisp.

By the time the fire department had arrived to put the fire out, Capt. Montgomery's body was a charred mess. They immediately declared the area a crime scene. Reporters were everywhere because it was a high-profile case. A high-ranked official was murdered, and they were now out for blood.

"That problem has been taken care of. You can breathe easy now."

"Check your mailbox after five this evening. Your package will be there. If I need you for anything else, I will contact you immediately."

"I hope it's all there, or I will be paying you a visit also."

"It will be all there! I went to the bank early this morning and withdrew the money. There was a new teller at the desk, so it took a little longer than normal, but I got it."

"Good, nice doing business with you."

The phone went dead, leaving the caller listening to silence. Three bulletproof SUVs pulled through the barricades, stopping in front of the scene. There were almost a hundred officers and FBI agents there that all stopped what they were doing and stood at attention when the doors to the vehicles opened. The mayor and police commissioner stepped out and headed for Capt. Montgomery's house. They were already informed of what they would be walking into and were fully prepared.

"Is there any way we can find out what was used to cause this before I leave?" the commissioner said to the fire marshal.

"It's going to take some time, sir. Our preliminary findings indicate some kind of professional pipe bomb," he replied.

"Okay, let me know something as soon as you can. I need some answers on what and who caused this!" the police commissioner told him, walking toward where Capt. Montgomery's fiancé was standing. "Mrs. Montgomery, I just wanted to say sorry for your loss. I know the detectives asked you questions already, but could I speak with you in private?"

The grieving lady nodded her head and led him toward the side entrance of the house so they could talk.

As soon as they entered the house, the lady walked into the kitchen and poured herself a cup of coffee. Commissioner Ray Ayers stood by the counter until she was done, and then removed his hat and glasses.

"Why the fuck did he die like that?" he yelled, punching the side of the counter, almost putting a hole through it.

"It was how you wanted it. You said you wanted a statement to be made and well . . ." she said, drying her eyes as if nothing had happened.

"Yeah, I did say that! Hopefully they will think that it was some gang bangers out for war against the police department. Did you give that package to the person you told me about?" he said, looking around to make sure no one was watching them.

"I did everything you said, and I even had an Oscar performance in front of those people out there," she smiled, moving closer to him.

She unzipped his pants and then stuck her hand inside, fondling his dick. As good as it felt, this wasn't the time. He pushed her hand away and fixed his pants.

"Don't do that!"

Tamara had been cheating on her husband for over a year with Capt. Montgomery. It had gotten so serious that he proposed to her and she said yes, even though she couldn't marry anyone else until she divorced her present husband. Ray had also been fucking her discretely just so he could use her to his own advantage.

She was a thick beauty. At age forty-nine, she still looked like she was in her late twenties, and even though she had picked up some extra pounds, men still wanted a piece of her sexual appetite. She has been on the city council committee since she was thirty. There was almost nothing that she couldn't make happen if asked, and that's why Ray had recruited her to hire one of her black-market assassins to put in some work.

"Will you come back tonight and stay with me?" she asked.

"I don't think I'll be able to make that kind of trip anytime soon, Tamara. There will be too much attention on you and your home," he replied.

"That never stopped you before," she said, thinking about how he would sneak into her home at night despite her fiancé sleeping in their bedroom.

"Look, Tamara, I have to be somewhere right now, but once again I'm really sorry for your loss," he sarcastically replied, heading for the door.

"You can't just leave me like this," Tamara started screaming. "If you don't come back here tonight, you will be sorry."

Ray's face turned beat red, and anger flowed freely through his body. As much as he wanted to snap out on her, he didn't because of all the unwanted attention outside the front of the house. It was at that moment that he knew Tamara would be a liability. Nothing was going to ruin what he had planned. He turned around and walked back over to where she was standing.

"We can meet up at the hotel tonight. Text me the room number, and I'll be there around eleven. Make sure you text it to my private number."

He gave her a kiss on the cheek and squeezed her ass. She gave him an approving smile and then watched as he walked out the door. He talked to his officers momentarily. Then he hopped in his vehicle and headed back to his office. He had an appointment to get ready for.

***

Symira stood in the mirror admiring her naked body and the baby growing in her stomach. She was starting to show now, and it was time to drop the news on Morgan. Every time she mustered up enough courage to tell him, he wouldn't answer his phone, so she decided that today she would just pop up at his office.

After she finished getting dressed, she grabbed her purse and left the hotel room. She dropped the key card off at the desk and then waited for her car to pull up. It only took her forty-five minutes to get to his office, being that she had arrived in Harrisburg the night before. When she walked into the building, all eyes were on her. She walked up to the desk demanding to see Morgan.

"I'm sorry, ma'am, but Governor Wright is very busy and asked not to be disturbed," the very sexy secretary told her.

"I don't care how busy he is; you tell him that the mother of his child wishes to see him right now."

The secretary looked at Symira, then at her stomach, with wide eyes. So, did everyone else that was watching the commotion. The secretary quickly paged the governor to deliver the message. Thirty seconds later, Morgan came rushing out of his office to see who was insinuating that he had a child. When he saw Symira standing there, he knew shit was about to hit the fan.

"Carmelita, hold all my calls and anything else until I let you know otherwise," he told her, and then led Symira back to his office.

Carmelita was a bit jealous after hearing that Symira was pregnant with Morgan's baby. Call it woman's intuition, but she had a feeling that she was trying to trap him with the baby. Carmelita had plans of doing something similar, but she was going to get money out of him by pretending to be pregnant. Now she would have to figure out another scheme to try to get what she wanted.

"What are you doing here?" Morgan asked, closing his office door behind them. "I told you that we couldn't be together anymore. Now you just pop up here after all this time carrying a baby and say that it's mine. How do I know you're not just saying that? Are you sure it's not Greg's baby?"

"Yes, I'm sure! The whole time we were fucking, I didn't have sex with him. You were the one who told me to fuck him, Morgan, so don't act like that."

"Look, I'm not trying to be rude or anything, but you had sex with someone who is HIV positive. You and the baby could be positive also."

"I have had numerous checkups with negative results every time. Do not try and put this all on me. We both played a part in all of this."

"I'm not putting it all on you, Symira. I just can't be sure until we get a paternity test to find out," he said, sitting down on the couch.

She sat down beside him hoping that she could persuade him to see the bright side of things. He watched her as she tried getting close to him, already knowing where this was heading. When she placed her hand on his leg, it confirmed what he already knew.

"Whoa, what are you doing?" Morgan asked, jumping up off the couch.

"I just wanted you to see what you're missing. Sit back down. I won't hurt you unless you want me to," she smiled, patting the seat next to her.

He had to admit to himself that he missed fucking her sexy body. He watched as she hiked her dress up, exposing her completely bald vagina. Symira hardly wore any panties unless she had to, and that was what he loved about her. He checked the door, making sure it was locked, and then walked over and stood in front of Symira.

She took that as her cue, unzipping his pants and removing his penis. Symira wrapped her lips around the tip, sending him into a frenzy. Morgan grabbed her head, then started fucking her face while playing with her titties.

"Ahhhh, yes, that feels so good," he said with his eyes closed.

Symira couldn't respond because her head was too busy moving back and forth, making loud slurping noises. She placed two fingers into her already dripping pussy and began playing with her clitoris. Morgan pulled back and lifted her up off the couch.

"Turn around and bend over. I need to see if you still feel the same."

Symira licked her lips, doing as she was told. She pulled the dress she was wearing all the way off, anticipating him penetrating her walls. Just as he aimed his dick at her hole, a warning sign flashed through his brain. He stopped in a hurry, reached into his pocket, and removed a condom. After strapping up, Morgan entered her from behind, pumping ferociously. Symira tried running from his thrust, but he had a hold on her waist like vise grips.

"This what you wanted? Huh?"

"Yes, fuck your pussy, baby, it's all yours," she screamed out.

Morgan knew that his behavior was very inappropriate, but at the moment it felt so right. It kind of reminded him of when they use to do this in his office. He pumped away until he finally exploded inside the condom. Symira felt him cum and tried to reach hers, but didn't.

"You have to help me now," she said, spreading her legs wider, inviting his tongue to handle its business.

"I can't do this right now, Symira. Fix yourself so we can talk about this baby situation, because I need to know everything," Morgan stated, pulling his pants up.

Symira was livid but didn't show any signs of it. She was still feeling really horny from the little sexcapade they just had. She stood up, fixed her dress, and then sat back down on the couch so they could have the highly-anticipated conversation. Morgan followed suit and sat next to her after pouring himself a drink.

They talked for about an hour trying to put everything into perspective. Carmelita was listening to the whole conversation on the intercom. She tried not to let the jealousy that was building up slip out. She didn't even know why she was feeling that way, because Morgan liked flirting with everyone. He had quite the reputation with the ladies, despite his political status. She blamed it on the fact that Symira was pregnant with his child.

"I'm going to set up an appointment with the doctor for tomorrow so that we can get this over with. I need to know if it's mine or not," Morgan told Symira.

"That's fine! Should I meet you there or will you send a car for me?"

"You can meet me here! I will have them perform the procedure in my office," he replied, not wanting the public to see him at a hospital getting a maternity test. "If this baby isn't mine, I want you out of my life."

"What if it is, Morgan?"

"Then I will give you enough money to get rid of it. That is the only solution that seems feasible."

"I'm not getting no fucking abortion," Symira said angrily.

"Symira how will it look if the news reporters find out that I had an affair on my wife and got you pregnant?"

"I don't care, and if it is yours and you try to make me get rid of it, I will take it public to the press. Your ass won't have to worry about politics anymore because your career will be over. I'll see you in the morning, Governor," Symira said, getting up off the couch.

Morgan jumped up to try to stop her from leaving, but she pushed him out of the way. Tears flowed freely down her face as she raced toward the elevator.

Morgan stood in his doorway watching her. Carmelita hit the button when she heard them coming out. She had her own thoughts racing through her mind.

"Maybe he will love me if I take care of the problem for him," she smiled to herself.

She began to formulate a plan in her head to get rid of Symira. When Morgan left out to use the restroom, Carmelita snuck into his office and searched through his phone until she found what she was looking for. She copied down the information and then left out before he returned.

"I'm feeling a bit under the weather right now! Do you mind if I leave early?" she asked Morgan when he came back.

"If all my appointments are rescheduled, you can take off, and I'll see you at seven o'clock tomorrow morning. We have a lot of work to do," he said, heading back in his office.

Carmelita smiled as she grabbed her purse and headed out. It was time to do some recon work on Symira because she was considered a threat to her happiness.

***

46

Michelle walked into the room to give Kevin his food. He hadn't eaten anything in two days because he was scared that she was trying to poison him. She smiled and then sat the McDonald's bag by his feet. When she removed the tape from his mouth, he moved it around trying to get some feeling back.

"You need to drink something before you become dehydrated," she said.

"I don't want nothing from you. Why are you holding me here, Michelle?" he said, turning his head away from the straw.

"If you eat something first, I'll explain everything to you," Michelle replied. She pulled the burger out of the wrapper and then placed it near his mouth. "Come on, honey, I know you're hungry!"

Kevin wanted to resist, but his stomach was screaming something else. He took a huge bite of the burger and chewed it cautiously, hoping it wasn't poisoned. Michelle then fed him the fries and apple pie and then let him wash it down with the soda. After he finished eating, she threw the trash in a plastic bag. Then she gave him a brief explanation of why he was there.

"To answer your question about why you're here, you are part of the ultimate plan. The world is gonna see you for your cheating, adulterating ways," she said, rubbing the side of his face.

"And how are you going to do that?"

"That, my dear, is part of the bigger plan, and you are not going to like the outcome. That is why I put a little something in your drink to help you."

"What did you give me?"

"Don't worry, nothing to kill you. I just gave you some molly to keep you at attention. I'm going to clean you up and get you ready for tonight," she said, dipping the washcloth into the bucket of water.

"What's supposed to happen tonight?"

"I get my life back and you . . . well, you'll find out," she told him, soaping up the rag.

Michelle quickly washed him up and then left him there with a stiff pecker while she went to get ready for the second part of her plan. There was another person that had tried to destroy her. Plus, she was planning to fuck him a few times to make it seem like he had raped and forced her to give him another baby. After that she was going to pop back up and say that he had faked her death and kept her locked inside a home. That she was able to escape captivity after persuading him to take the rope from around her hands, with the promise of not trying to run.

She had formulated the perfect story and had it down to a T. The only problem was the resentment she might have to face from her son for killing his deceitful father. He was going to take the loss of his dad very hard. Not only did she have to worry about Mike though. There was Sahmeer as well, because she knew that Kevin was his father also. Michelle had been spying on them for quite some time now. That was one of the main reasons she was doing this.

"Pretty soon I will be able to live my life like I deserve, and that no-good cheating bastard won't be laughing at me anymore," she mumbled to herself.

She made sure her fake wig was on right, grabbed her purse, and then left out to perform the second part of her plan. This was the hardest, but yet most important part if she wanted everything to go smoothly. Michelle had one other person that needed to join the party, and she knew just how to get their attention.

***

"I still can't figure out why he hasn't showed up to his new team or answered his phone," Marcus said, talking to Sasha on the phone.

He was sitting in the locker room getting ready for his game. They were about to play Golden State, and this was supposed to be Kevin's debut with them.

"That's not like him, Marcus. Even if he was mad at you, he would at least answer one of your calls, not to mention, show up to his game. That boy loves playing basketball!" she replied.

"Go back to their house and check with Mike. See if he talked to him. I have to go now, our warm ups are about to start. Just leave me a text message, and I will check it at halftime. Love you!"

"I'll go over there when I get out of the shower," she told him. "Love you too!"

Sasha disconnected their call and then removed her robe to get in the shower. That was the first time in a while she had heard those words. It was like music to her ears, and she blushed.

After she got out of the shower, she threw on a pair of sweatpants and a sweater and then headed over to Kevin's house. When she got there, she knocked on the door a few times but got no answer.

It was kind of dark, so she couldn't look through the window. She walked to the back to retrieve the spare key they kept under the doormat.

Sasha walked inside and hit the light switch, but nothing happened. A feeling of caution suddenly hit her, so she turned to leave. Before she could get to the door, someone grabbed her from behind, covering her mouth with their hand. Sasha frantically tried to break free, but couldn't. She was scared for her life as the intruder pulled her back further into the house. Her life was flashing before her eyes.

"Shhhhhh, I'm not going to hurt you," the person whispered in her ear.

She immediately recognized the voice and then broke free. When she turned around, it wasn't the person she thought it was.

"What the hell—" she began to say.

"Calm down. I think somebody was in the house. I came here to see if Kevin was here, but this is how everything looked," Sahmeer stated, pointing to the destroyed furniture and broken glass.

"Boy, you scared the shit out of me," Sasha replied, calming down.

"Sorry about that, mom. I'm just worried about Mike and Kevin. Who would do this, and how did they get through the security check-in?"

"I don't know, but we should get out of this place just in case they come back," Sasha said, walking toward the door.

"You go ahead. I'm going to stick around and try to straighten up a bit. If someone comes back, I'll call the police."

"I'm going back home, but be careful, and if you hear anything, please let me know," Sasha said, leaving out.

As she walked past the garage door, she felt a sharp sting on the side of her neck. She tried to reach for it, but felt dizzy. Before she could say anything, she fell to the ground. All she saw was a face before blacking out.

FOUR

"OKAY, CLASS, SETTLE DOWN," the college professor said to his students when he walked into the classroom.

They all calmed down, sat in their chairs, and waited for further instructions. Veronica and her best friend, Ariana, were still whispering about the party that they were going to throw tonight for the beginning of spring break. They couldn't wait until the rest of their classes were over.

"If you ladies are done chatting, I would like to start teaching my class. Ms. Davis, if I were you, I would definitely be paying attention to what's going on, considering your last test grade."

"Sorry, Mr. Kessler," she flirtatiously replied, biting her bottom lip.

There were a bunch of snickers from her classmates, but it quickly silenced when Steven gave them a crazy look. All the girls in Temple University had a school girl crush on Mr. Kessler. He knew it, but it never bothered him at all because he had no intentions of crossing that line.

At the age of thirty-six, Steven Kessler was the youngest college professor in the school. He had recently married his girlfriend after being together for a year and a half. She was a housewife but traveled back and forth to help her parents, who resided in Miami, Florida, with the family business. They would hardly see each other during the week. His class consisted of about seventy-five students, and they all came from parents with some kind of ties to the school. There were times when he would wonder why some of them decided to attend this school instead of some ivy-league college, because they were very intelligent students. Everyone except Veronica!

"Thank you! Now I want everyone to design a web page and divide the image into slices, add links and HTML text, optimize the slices, and then save it. That will tell me who's been paying attention or not," he stated.

"What are slices?" Veronica whispered to Ariana.

"Girl, are you serious?"

"Yes, girl, you know I never focus while I'm here," Veronica replied, giving her friend a devilish smile.

Ariana already knew what that meant. They shared everything, so there weren't any secrets that were kept from each other. Veronica's crush for her teacher went as far as her having fantasies and daydreams of him fucking her in the classroom. That's the reason she never paid attention in class.

"If you want to pass this class, I suggest you start," she giggled.

"Bitch, that's why I got you!" Veronica smirked.

"A slice is the rectangular area of an image that you can use to create links, rollovers, and animations in the web page. Dividing an image into slices lets you selectively optimize it for web viewing. I thought you knew how to do that."

"So, I can basically download faster by using slices?"

"You know what, I knew your crazy ass could do it," Ariana said, throwing a balled-up piece of paper at Veronica.

They laughed and then started their work. Mr. Kessler gave them about forty minutes to complete the assignment and then made everyone stop. He walked around each desk and checked the work. When he approached Veronica's desk, she barely was halfway done.

"Ms. Davis, did you understand what I asked you to do?"

"No, I got stuck after the first part," she said in a frustrated tone.

Before he could reply, the bell rang indicating class was over. He walked back toward the front of the classroom while everyone gathered up their belongings.

"I will see you after spring break. Enjoy yourselves, and for most of you, at least try to stay out of trouble," he smirked, causing some of them to laugh. "Ms. Davis, I would like to speak with you for a brief moment."

"Uh oh, you're about to get spanked across the desk for being a naughty girl," Ariana joked. "Call me when you get home so we can head over to the club and make sure everything is ready for tonight."

"Okay, see you later, bitch," she said.

Ariana stuck her middle finger out and left out the classroom. Veronica sat at one of the desks in the front row, waiting to see why Mr. Kessler wanted to talk to her. He sat down at his desk and removed his glasses.

"Listen, you are a bright student, and I really don't want to fail you, but you're leaving me no choice in the matter. This was one of the easiest assignments that I gave out this year, yet you still couldn't get it done in a reasonable amount of time. Is there something going on that I should know about?"

"No! I just didn't understand it at first, but I will do it when I get home and send it to your e-mail," she said, crossing her legs, but not too fast, trying to give him a glimpse of her lace panties.

He noticed what she did, and quickly refocused his eyes on something else. He stood up and gathered all of his paperwork so he could head out to pick up his wife from the airport. The excitement in his pants was very noticeable, but he covered it well with his briefcase.

"I will be expecting that e-mail soon if you want to pass this semester. Thank you for staying back," he said, walking her to the door.

"Is that all you wanted?" she asked in a flirting manner.

"What do you mean?"

Veronica could see that he wasn't going for the bait, so she didn't reply. She placed her bag over her shoulders and walked out in front of him, swaying her hips side to side.

"If you're not doing anything tonight, why don't you come to 8th Street Lounge. We are throwing a spring break party there. I think you will have fun," she said as they walked down the hall.

He stopped and then turned to her. "Veronica, I cannot be out at some club fraternizing with my students. I could get in a lot of trouble, so thanks but no thanks, I'll pass."

"I didn't mean it like that," she said. "It's just a regular over-twenty-one club, full of regular people, but suit yourself. Have a good vacation, Mr. Kessler, and check your e-mail by seven," she said smiling.

Steven walked out to his car and rushed off to pick up his wife. He needed some well-deserved alone time with her, and tonight he was going to fuck her brains out. He smiled at that thought while hitting the gas pedal.

Veronica also headed home, with a different mission in mind. Instead of sending just the homework assignment, she planned on sending him a nice video. She figured once he saw it, he wouldn't look at her as a little girl anymore. She turned on one of her favorite songs and sang along as she cruised down the expressway.

I got all exotic bitches, you gone think I'm racist, I just called a gang of bitches out of immigration. You gone think we printing money cause of when we make it, I got all these fucking wheels and ain't got no payments. Pink slip sitting in the dashboard wit me, gotta gang of broads riding and their on drugs wit me, gotta gang of cash on me like I brought the plug wit me. Looking for

the plug, I'm the plug really! Really,
I'm the plug, Really, I'm the plug . . .

***

Steven and his wife sat on the living room couch watching the new version of Apollo, hosted by Steve Harvey. When it went off, he thought that now was the time to make his move. He started kissing Monica's neck trying to get her in the mood.

"Let's go upstairs and take a hot shower, and then I'll rub you down with your favorite lotion," he whispered in her ear.

"I don't feel like it right now. I had a long flight. All I want to do is take a shower alone and get some rest."

"I thought we were going to have fun tonight since we haven't seen each other all week?"

"We will, just not tonight! We can do whatever you like tomorrow. I'll see you when you come upstairs," she said, giving him a peck on the lips. "Don't forget to take the trash out and lock up before you come up."

"I got this, you do whatever you want," he replied, keeping his cool.

He took the trash out, locked up, grabbed a couple of beers out of the refrigerator, and then headed up to the bedroom. Fifteen minutes later, Monica came out of the bathroom dripping wet, with only a towel on. She sat on the side of the bed and then put on her panty and bra set. Steven had a full erection by now and wanted some pussy. When Monica lay back in the bed, he moved behind her letting his erection rest on her ass cheeks. He tried to grind on her, but she cut it short.

"I said not tonight, Steven, I'm tired."

"This is so crazy. Why is it that every time I want to be with you, you're all of a suddenly tired? You know what, never mind, don't answer that. I'll be downstairs," Steven said, walking out of the room.

"Steven!" she called out, but he didn't answer.

He turned on his laptop, deciding to catch up on some work. He checked his e-mails and noticed that he had two from Veronica. When he opened the first one, it was her completed assignment, so he graded it and sent it back. The second one was a one-minute video clip, so he opened it up. What he saw, shocked him. It was a video of her doing a striptease. He quickly turned it off, but didn't delete it. He finished off his second beer and then started putting together a lesson plan for after the break.

He heard his wife's phone go off, and looked at it sitting on the table. When he looked at the screen, it was a text message from someone named Morgan. Curiosity got the best of him, and he opened the text and read it. His heart almost jumped out of his body after he read the message. He ran up the steps with her phone in hand.

"Who the fuck is this?" he said, tossing Monica the phone.

She looked at the text and was speechless. She wasn't expecting him to go through her phone, because he had never done that before. Now she had to figure out how to explain herself.

"What does he mean, he has a surprise for you when you get back and that he misses you so much?" Steven asked, waiting for an answer.

"That was one of my coworkers playing with me. He always sends one of the workers a text like that. Baby, he is gay and only likes men," she said, trying to defuse the situation.

"Look, I really don't know what to believe right now. I need to get some air to clear my head," he said, putting some clothes on and leaving the room.

He grabbed his laptop and car keys and then left the house. He sat in his car for a few minutes, leaning his head back against the headrest. His thoughts drifted off to one of his students and their discussion from earlier. Steven opened up his computer and then clicked on the e-mail that his student had sent to him. It was very sensual and aroused him instantly. Veronica danced for the camera and stripped all the way down to her panties and bra, before turning the camera off.

Steven closed the computer, sat it to the side, and then started his vehicle. He decided to stop by the club Veronica said they would be at. Since he was dressed for the occasion, he came to the conclusion that it wasn't going to hurt anyone because it was a public spot.

When Steven arrived at the club, he paid at the door and then headed inside. It was dark and packed, so he walked over to the bar, where he found a seat.

"What you having?" the bartender asked.

"I'll take a rum and coke, with a double shot of rum."

The bartender left to retrieve his drink. Steven looked around at all the pretty women dancing on the floor or drinking while conversing with friends. His eyes stopped on the three beautiful women dancing in the middle of the crowd. After focusing his eyes from the lighting in the room, he realized that it was Veronica, Ariana, and another girl. He watched them dance together for three songs before he and Veronica locked eyes. She stopped dancing and made her way toward him.

"Mr. Kessler, you came," she said, giving him a more than friendly hug.

"I just came to check out the scenery. I see you know how to dance."

"You haven't seen nothing yet. Come with me, Mr. Kessler," Veronica said, grabbing him by the hand and leading him out on the dance floor.

He pulled his hand back and stopped in mid-stride. "Stop calling me that! While I'm here, call me Steven, okay?"

"Whatever you say, Steven."

Veronica escorted him to the middle of the floor and then started grinding against his body. Steven grabbed her by the waist, pulling her even closer into his embrace. She wrapped her arms around his neck, and they danced in rhythm to the music. Ariana and her girlfriend watched them moving in sync with each other.

"Isn't that y'all computer lab teacher that V is dancing with?" Lala asked.

"Yeah, that's him, girl. She's been flirting with his ass all year."

"I guess she finally got what she wanted, huh?" Lala mumbled as if she was jealous.

"Come on, let's go say hello," Ariana said, pulling Lala toward the dance floor where Steven and Veronica were.

Steven's hands were all over Veronica's ass, and it looked as if he were playing with her pussy. Lala touched his shoulder, causing him to jump. They stopped dancing and smiled at the two girls.

"How are you, Mr. Kessler? What, you wanted to come party with your students?" Lala asked sarcastically, waiting for a response.

"I was supposed to meet a couple of friends, but they bailed on me at the last minute," he lied, trying to save face. He didn't want to get snitched on, so he decided to leave. "Well, ladies, I have to get out of here. Drive safe and make sure one of you is the designated driver."

Steven rushed up out of there, thinking about how he was rubbing on his student's body. She felt and smelled so good.

"Why did you say that?" Veronica snapped at Lala.

"I was just playing!"

"Damn it, Lala, I'll be right back, and you owe me a drink, bitch, so go get it," she yelled over the music.

She ran outside looking around for Steven. She spotted him walking toward the parking lot and ran after him.

"Steven, wait up," she said, finally catching up with him.

Steven stopped once he reached his car, and then removed his keys to disarm his car alarm. He hopped inside and was ready to start the engine, when Veronica snatched the key from him.

"Why did you just leave like that? I had a special treat for you."

"And what was that?" he asked, curiosity overwhelming him.

"Sit right there and I'll show you. Let the roof down on your car," she told him, walking in front of the car.

He did as he was told and let the roof down. Veronica removed her panties, climbed on top of the hood, and stood in front of where he was sitting. She lifted her skirt above the waist, exposing her clean-shaved vagina, and then did a split right on the window shield. She started to rub her pussy as she pulled one of her breasts out and sucked on her own nipple.

Steven was so turned on that he didn't even realize he had unzipped his pants and pulled out his penis. He started massaging it while watching her do her thing. When Veronica came, her juices flowed down the window. She eased off the car and walked around to the passenger seat.

"I see someone enjoyed the show," she chuckled devilishly, staring at his rock-hard penis. "Let me help you with that."

She replaced his hand with hers and started jerking his dick nice and slow. Steven's eyes closed immediately as her touch drove him over the edge. His load shot out all over the steering wheel and dashboard. Some even got on his pants. He reached over and stuck a finger inside her pussy, causing her to let out a soft moan. Before he got the chance to go any further, Veronica's cell phone rang.

"I'm coming," she said softly into the phone. Unbeknownst to her friends, she was literally cumming, but it was all over Steven's fingers.

Steven realized what he was doing and stopped, pulling his hand away from her. He zipped his pants up, letting Veronica know that their fun had come to a sudden halt.

"I think you should be getting back to your friends, 'cause I have to get home to my wife. She's probably looking for me right now," he chuckled.

"We definitely have to finish this one day," she said, leaning over, giving him a kiss on the cheek, and then stepping out of the car.

"You're forgetting something," he told her, pointing to her panties that were left on the seat.

"You keep them to remember this moment."

She closed the door and rushed back inside to her friends. Steven looked at the clock, noticing that it was now 1:38 a.m. He headed home hoping that she was still sleeping. While he was on I-76, he tossed Veronica's underwear out the window. He wasn't stupid enough to take them back home.

When he got home, he took a quick shower and slid into bed without her even noticing. He lay there thinking about Veronica until he dozed off. Monica's eyes popped open, and she looked over to her husband, whose back was toward her, and then looked at the clock. She had gone downstairs looking for him earlier, but he wasn't there. So, her suspicions were confirmed when he went straight to the shower as soon as he got home.

She thought he was out cheating on her because he saw the text from the guy that she was having an affair with. Monica had a feeling that their marriage was doomed once she started catching feelings for Morgan. It wasn't supposed to happen, but it did, and now she was in a bit of a predicament. She decided that she would deal with it when the time was right. She texted someone and then fell asleep waiting for a response.

FIVE

SASHA WOKE UP FEELING groggy from whatever had been injected into her neck. She suddenly started to panic because she could hear someone breathing heavily next to her. It was too dark to make out the figure, but she could tell that they were also sleeping. Her mouth was covered with duct tape, and her hands and legs were bound together, so she couldn't yell out for help. The place she was in had a musty smell to it, which made her realize she was in someone's basement. She started shaking trying to break free, but to no avail. It only made her wrists hurt more from the bounds.

"Mmmmm, mmmmm, mmmmm," she kept trying to scream, but nothing came out.

"There's no use in screaming 'cause no one can hear you," a voice calmly explained to her. She looked around panicking, trying to see who it was.

"Mmmmmmmmm!"

"Don't worry, Sasha, you will see me soon enough. If I were you, I would be saving all of my energy 'cause your gonna need it," the voice said once again.

At that moment, Sasha knew exactly who it was that had her captive. Just the sound of the voice had her paranoid about what was to come. She was so scared that she peed on herself. To say her past had come back to haunt her was an understatement. When he removed the tape from her mouth, Sasha started screaming.

"Help! Somebody please help me!"

The man smacked the shit out of Sasha, silencing her cries for help. He put his hands around her throat and squeezed, causing her face to turn colors.

"I remember when you used to love this," he cried. "Now look at your rich and famous ass, begging for air. I want the rest of my fucking money."

He released his grip, waiting for an answer. Sasha coughed trying to get some air into her lungs. She was not expecting to ever see this man again.

"How did you find me, and what are you talking about? I paid you all the money I owed," she said, shaking.

"See, that's where your wrong, Sasha," he shot back. "That money you paid me was only hush money to keep me quiet while I was sitting behind bars. You and everyone else thought I was going to rot in a prison cell, but here I am. When I took that case for you, you told me that I wouldn't have to worry about nothing. You put five hundred dollars on my books and never sent another dime. I tried reaching out to you, but your phone number was changed."

"It wasn't on purpose, I swear. I was trying to find a job first, and then I was going to—"

"Stop lying, bitch," he shouted, smacking the shit out of her. "You left me for dead thinking that I wouldn't be able to get to you. Do you have any idea what it was like to be assaulted every night against my will? Do you?"

"Please, I didn't know. Just let me go, and I'll give you more money," she pleaded.

"Oh, so now I have the upper hand, huh? Well, I want you to make sure that you know that I really do. There's someone I want you to meet," he stated matter of factly.

The light suddenly came on, and Sasha damn near puked at the sight of the badly beaten body sitting five feet away from her. Upon further observation, she realized that it was Kevin. His face was swollen, and he had lacerations all over his naked body.

"Oh, my God, Kevin!"

"He wouldn't tell me where his money was, so hopefully you won't give us that same problem."

"Who is *us*?" she questioned, wanting to know who his accomplice was.

"Don't worry about it. This is what you're going to do without saying another word, or you will end up like him," he stated, pointing to Kevin. "You're gonna give me your account information, and I'm going to pay a visit to your bank to clean it out."

"They will never let you withdraw that much money without me or my husband being present," she said, trying to minimize the situation.

"I thought you would say that, so I came prepared," he replied, pulling out a piece of paper.

"What is that?"

"This is a Power of Attorney form. Sign it, and once I get what I want, you can be on your way," he told her.

"I'm not going to sign that," she snapped.

"Wrong answer," he said, pulling out a 9mm pistol.

Without hesitating, he shot Kevin in his kneecaps twice. Sasha screamed out in horror as she watched him squealing in pain. His sounds were muffled from the duct tape covering his mouth.

"Are you going to sign it or do I have to kill him this time?"

Sasha and everybody else thought Kevin had just up and left without saying anything, and now here it was that he had really been kidnapped. She wondered why they weren't trying to take his money. He was a millionaire with a lot more money than she would ever see. The only reason she was living fabulously was because of her husband's wealth. She thought back to the day when Brian took the wrap for the drugs that were found inside her trunk:

(February 18, 1997)

"All you have to do is drop this work off on your way back to school. They will pass you a yellow envelope with twenty grand inside. Just hold onto it until your lunch break, and I will come pick it up from you then," Akbar said, passing Sasha the book bag with the heroin inside.

She and her friend Michelle were planning to go watch their friends play their last game before March Madness started. They had had their eyes on these two young men since the beginning of the season. Sasha's only problem was that she had a jealous boyfriend that would do anything for her, but she was tired of his possessive ways.

"Okay, let me get out of here. I'll call you after my second class, so make sure you be there on time," she replied, walking out the door. Akbar watched her ass jiggle from side to side as she shut the door behind her.

When she stepped inside the car, Brian pulled off. They drove down Master Street listening to Jay Z's

Hard Knock Life Vol 2 CD. Sasha was happy that she was making money from it.

"Look at this, babe," she said, removing a pack of the dope from the book bag.

"Put that shit up before you get us busted," Brian snapped.

She put the drugs up and threw the book bag in the backseat. They pulled into the gas station on 52nd and Master to get gas. Sasha stayed in the car while Brian paid for the gas and grabbed two Dutches. Five minutes later, they were cruising down the avenue toward their destination. They arrived on Mellon Street ten minutes later.

"I'm a take it in for you. I'm not feeling all these niggas hanging out around that crib," he stated, reaching for the bag.

"No, I got it. They are expecting me to come. That's why Akbar asked me."

"I said I will take it. Something just don't seem right," he snapped. Sasha was about to say something, but the look he gave her made her change her mind. "I'll be right back!"

Brian made sure his gun was tucked in his waist. He then stepped out of the car. He walked past the group of men standing on the porch and went inside the house. Sasha sat there looking out the window, hoping he didn't try to steal from the envelope. She knew he wouldn't, but the thought still crossed her mind. She loved him, but she wasn't trying to be stuck in the hood all her life. She had plans on being some rich man's wife, and it was going to happen one way or the other. That was the reason her and Michelle took a liking to Kevin and Marcus. They saw the potential in them and knew that one day they would be NBA stars.

She looked at the clock realizing that Brian had been inside for over ten minutes. It usually only took five. Out of nowhere, six undercover cars stormed the block. Everyone scattered trying to get away. Sasha jumped out of the car, grabbing her purse and phone, and then ran down the street and sat on a stranger's porch. Keeping her eyes on the porch, she watched as the cops walked out holding the book bag that Brian went in with, and dragging Brian out with cuffs on his wrist.

"Oh, my God. What the fuck?" she said, watching the cops place Brian in the car. She needed to get out of there before she ended up going to jail, so she headed for the avenue to find a taxi. She couldn't take the car because they were now searching it.

***

Three hours later, Sasha and Michelle sat in the house listening to music when her cell phone rang. She answered it, wondering who the strange number was. Her question was answered as soon as she heard the voice on the other end.

"You need to get me the fuck out of here, Sasha," Brian demanded.

"How much is your bail?"

"Two hundred thousand," he said.

"I don't have that kind of money. What am I supposed to do?"

"I don't care what you do. Go sell your ass or something. Just get me the fuck out of here. I took the rap for your shit, and you best to do something to make it right."

"I will try to help you out, but don't make it seem like it's my fault. I told you to let me go in, but you insisted on doing it. I'm going to ask my peoples to get you out," Sasha said.

"Phone call's over," the officer yelled in the background.

"Just handle this shit, or we're going to have a problem," Brian replied, hanging up in her ear. Sasha looked at her phone in disbelief, but at the same time she was happy that she wasn't the one who had to go to prison. She was going to talk to her friend to get Brian a lawyer for his case, but decided not to. Instead, she sent Brian a five-hundred-dollar money order from her college fund hoping that he wouldn't bitch, but boy was she wrong. He called her so much that she changed her number to avoid him. Her thoughts were that he was going to be down for a very long time. Now she could focus on Marcus, because unlike Brian, he had a promising career. She knew that he was destined to become an NBA star. He was going to be her meal ticket out of the hood. She just had to figure out a way to trap him up. She decided that she would do whatever needed to be done.

"Are you going to answer me, or do I have to put a bullet through his skull?" Brain asked again, pointing the gun at Kevin's head.

Sasha snapped back to reality from her daydream, looking up at the weapon aimed at Kevin's head. She was scared to death, wondering how Brian got out of jail.

"Please don't do this. I can't authorize you to withdraw that kind of money from my husband's account. Let me go, and I can get it myself because the bank knows me."

"You know, Sasha, you're such a good liar. What did you think, that the twenty years I spent in prison made me unaware of the new technology today? Well, it only made me that much smarter, my dear. You're married without a prenuptial agreement, which means you have all access to any if not all of his accounts, like him. Now sign the fucking paper and stop trying to insult my intelligence, okay?"

When she still didn't move, Brian squeezed the trigger, shooting Kevin at point-blank range, in the back of the head. Sasha screamed as the tears ran freely down her face. Different thoughts started to flow through her head, like why was he here in the first place. He wasn't her husband, and what were his dealings with Brian? It even crossed her mind that maybe Marcus had caught them still sneaking around, but brushed that theory off quickly. She would never get the chance to ask him.

Brian unwrapped Sasha's writing hand and passed her a pen. Without saying a word, she signed the Power of Attorney form, defeated.

"Why couldn't you have just done that the first time?" he said, taping her hand back up. "I'm going to the bank, and if this works, I'll send a text to my partner and he will let you go. If anything goes wrong though, I'll be the last face you'll ever see."

He called out to somebody, and two people walked down the steps. After barking some orders, they carried Sasha up the steps and sat her in the living room.

"You stay with this bitch, and you come with me," Brian said, heading toward the door.

He turned around and whispered something to the guy staying behind, and then he walked out. The guy sat on the couch in front of Sasha and just stared at her. Even with her face beet red from being smacked, he still thought she was beautiful. He walked into the kitchen and poured some ice into one of the kitchen cloths, and then he walked back where Sasha was, placing the ice over her face.

"Thank you," she said. "He's going to kill me, ain't he?"

The look the guy gave her said it all. She needed to figure out a way out of there, and fast. After holding the ice on her face for a while, he put a piece of tape over her mouth and then went upstairs. A thousand questions fluttered through her mind as she looked around trying to find a way out of there. He came back down with a bucket of soapy water.

"You stink, so I'm going to wash you up real quick. It really doesn't matter because you're not going anywhere, but you're too pretty to smell like piss," he told her.

Sasha watched as he began washing her legs, working his way up. When he reached between her legs, she jumped, trying to close them as much as she could. He pulled them back open and ripped her panties off. She felt his hand rubbing against her pussy with the warm rag, and closed her eyes. She could tell that he was enjoying himself, so she thought that maybe she could use his lust to her advantage.

"Mmmmmmm," she moaned, opening her legs, trying to get his attention.

She could tell that he was liking the way her moist spot felt by the way he paid extra attention to it. She kept moving her head trying to get his attention. To her, he looked no more than about twenty five years old. It would be easy to manipulate him into doing what she wanted. What he didn't know was, the power of the pussy is very real.

"What is it?" he asked, sitting the rag down and then removing the tape so she could speak.

"Listen, I like the way you were just touching me. Why don't you take this tape off so I can show my appreciation?" He started contemplating it momentarily, so Sasha decided to keep going with her plan. "I could tell that you were enjoying it too. They won't be back for a while, so we can enjoy this together."

She could see that he definitely was liking the idea by the bulge in his pants. He whipped out a switchblade from his back pocket and started cutting the tape from her arms and legs. When he finished, Sasha stood up to stretch.

"Can you make love to me since this may be the last time I get to have sex?" she pleaded.

He sat down on the couch and removed his clothes. He watched as she unbuttoned her skirt, allowing it to fall down to the floor, revealing her naked body. His dick immediately began responding to the events that were ready to take place.

When she made it over to him, she spun around and showed off her assets. He licked his lips and squeezed her ass. Sasha scooted between his legs and placed her hand on his shaft, stroking it up and down until it was fully erect.

"Are you ready for me to taste this big cock of yours?" she teased, biting her bottom lip. He nodded his head and leaned back, waiting for her to wrap those lips around his dick.

She massaged his scrotum again, tracing each ball with her fingertips. He enjoyed her touch and sighed from the pleasure that came from her touch. Under normal circumstances, this would have had Sasha's pussy soaked, but this was about survival. When he closed his eyes again, she opened her mouth wide and bit down into his penis with immense force. She pressed down hard on his dick, grinding her teeth while shaking her head frantically from side to side like a predator devouring its prey. He squealed like a slaughtered hog and fell off the couch in pain.

"You sick, perverted muthafucka," she screamed, kicking him in the chest and face. He balled up in a fetal position.

She saw his knife on the floor and picked it up. He was in so much pain that he didn't even see it coming until it plunged into his stomach. Sasha hurried to put her clothes back on and then searched for a way to get out of the house. Blood was still all over her face from her biting technique, so she used the tablecloth from the kitchen table to wipe it off. While he was still squirming around on the ground, she searched his pockets and found his car keys. She ran out of the house, hopped in the car, and sped off searching for the police.

As Sasha sped off, another car pulled up. Michelle got out of the car and headed inside the house. What she saw made her start panicking.

"What the . . . ?" she said, looking at the dead body on the floor.

She immediately rushed down into the basement to check on Kevin and Sasha. When she saw Kevin lying on the floor with a bullet hole to the head, she lost it. She grabbed his body and held him, crying her heart out. Her plan had just been compromised. She looked around for Sasha's body, but couldn't find her. Her sixth sense immediately went off, informing her that she needed to get out of there fast.

Before she could get out, she heard fast-approaching sirens. She had to think on the fly, so she ran upstairs, ripped her clothes, and then pulled out the restraints that she was supposed to use on Sasha. Next, she picked up a heavy vase and broke it over her head. She tied the restraints on her legs, taped her mouth, and then cuffed herself to the bed.

When the cops found Michelle tied up, all hell broke loose. Everyone thought she was dead, and here she was in the flesh. She told the reporters that she had been held captive all this time. They needed to know how, so there were questions after questions about the kidnapping. When Sasha saw her best friend, she broke out in tears.

"I can't believe it's really you. Why did they do this?" she asked.

"I don't know! I have been there ever since though."

***

They were at the hospital because the detectives insisted on Michelle getting checked out. Because of her husband's celebrity status, this became a high-profile case. The feds had arrived to speak with her, but she still didn't have any new information for them. In fact, she didn't want to say anything because if they caught the people involved, she would be implicated also. Michelle's only option was to eliminate anything that would lead back to her.

"Sasha, I tried so many times to get away, but I couldn't. What was Kevin doing there, and why did they kill him?" she said, starting to sob.

"Everyone is trying to figure that out, Michelle. He went missing the night before he was supposed to go to his new team. Every time we called him, we got his voicemail. Marcus received a text message from him saying that he needed time to himself, but that was it."

"They killed him, Sasha. They shot my husband in cold blood," she pretended to be oblivious to the whole thing.

Michelle could have won an Oscar for the performance she was putting on. If anyone knew that she was actually the brains behind the whole thing, she would be locked under the jail. The feds questioned Sasha and Michelle for hours trying to figure out who was behind it all, but they couldn't get any more information out of them. The feds were under the assumption that whoever the last person was, they were now far away.

"I called Mike and Marcus. They are on their way here now. I tried to explain it to them, but I thought it would be better in person," Sasha said, rubbing her friend's head.

"Thank you, Sasha, for saving me."

"Michelle, just get some rest," Sasha replied, watching her friend doze off from the medicine that they put in her IV.

If Sasha hadn't escaped, they probably wouldn't have known that Michelle was even there, better yet, still alive.

SIX

STEVEN WAS IN HIS class going over his lesson plans
for the rest of the week. Spring break was over, and
he had to make sure that everything was in order. It
was getting late, so he decided to wrap things up for
the night and get home to the empty house that
awaited him. As he was getting ready to leave, he
heard his classroom door open. He looked up and
saw Veronica standing there.

"Ms. Davis, what are you doing here?"

"I came to see you, Mr. Kessler. I knew you
would be back early, so I thought maybe we could
finish what we started the last time I was here with
you alone."

Veronica made her way over until she and Steven
came face to face. As he stared down at her, he

couldn't help but notice how innocent and beautiful she looked. She really possessed perfect features, nothing too big or too small. Steven had never thought he would cheat on his wife, but Veronica was becoming very tempting to him. She had no scars, no pimples or blemishes on her body. To top it off, her eyes were mesmerizing. Steven leaned forward and kissed her on the lips.

"I know it's wrong for us to get involved with each other, it's just something about you. I need to know why you keep trying to come on to me. Is it because I'm the key to whether you pass or fail?" he asked, holding her waist.

"No, it's because I find you extremely sexy and I love the fact that you're married. It means that anything we do comes with no strings attached."

Steven stepped back until he came in contact with the edge of his desk, and then he sat on it. He looked Veronica up and down, studying her body.

"Take your clothes off."

She was somewhat surprised at his request, especially being in school. Yet she didn't hesitate to oblige. She made sure they were alone and then unbuttoned her blouse and took it off, hanging it on the black of the chair. She pulled her jeans off next, leaving them on the floor.

"Leave them on," he told her when she started pulling down her panties.

Veronica did as she was told, reaching behind her back, unfastening her bra, and tossing it on the chair with her blouse. She was very good at the art of seduction. She had used it on him before, but this time she was going to take total control of the situation, so she thought. Slowly, she sauntered over to him, taking notice of his eyes darting back and forth all over her perfect body. Lust enveloped his face as she planned to give him the business.

"Come here," he demanded, sitting in his chair.

Not wasting her time waiting for him to repeat his self, she straddled him. To cut all the conversation, she began kissing him, their tongues roaming each other's mouths vigorously. She lifted his Polo shirt over his head and then tossed it on the floor, thrusting her tongue back into his mouth. Steven's hands began to explore her body until they came to her firm ass, where he squeezed and massaged it. His tongue made its way across her cheek, down to her neck, shoulders, and collarbone, and then stopped at her soft perky breasts. Her hardened nipples alone gave him the satisfaction he was looking for.

He licked and sucked her breasts while Veronica moaned, groaned, and pressed her soaking wet pussy against his hard-on that couldn't wait to be released from the confinements of his pants. He placed his hands under her arms and lifted her up on the desk. Steven stood up and stepped in between her legs, continuing to kiss her. His lips slid down over her chin and breasts and past her stomach, and found their way to her womanhood, where he wasted no time diving in face first. Steven was no slouch when it came to oral sex.

"Oh shit, eat my pussy, baby," she said, spreading her legs wider for him to have easier access to her love tunnel.

His tongue traveled inside and out of her hole in search of her G-spot. The more his lips and fingers caressed her pussy, the more her body squirmed.

"You like that, don't you?" he asked, coming up for air.

"Ummm hmmm," was all she could say, grabbing his head and pushing it back between her legs.

Her moans got louder with every flick of his tongue. This went on for a good fifteen to twenty minutes before Steven stood up and removed his pants and boxers, exposing his nine-and-a-half-inch python. As he was doing so, Veronica started pulling off her panties, then massaging her pussy lips and playing with her nipples. He was shocked when she brought her fingers up from her wetness and slid them into her mouth.

"Please, I want that big dick inside me now," she moaned, staring at his stiffness pointing directly at her.

Hearing that, Steven pulled her body to the edge of the desk, stood between her legs, and then commenced to rubbing his dick up and down her slit until she reached out, grabbed ahold of it, and slowly guided the head inside of her. He gripped both of her legs and slowly stroked in and out of her slippery hole. He was thrown off by how tight it was the deeper he went.

Unaware of the fact that she hadn't had sex in a while, he picked up the pace, trying to knock her back out. Veronica screamed out in ecstasy. It was a combination of both pleasure and pain. Her pussy was on fire from the pounding it was enduring. He was able to hit every nerve inside her with his method in which he rotated and kept switching his strokes up on her. He placed her legs up on his shoulders and went to work on her pussy, hurting her even more.

Veronica felt him in places she thought only gynecologist knew about. Without a doubt, he had found her spot, because Veronica started trembling and cumming all over his dick. Steven was sweating profusely as tears of joy and pain ran down the side of Veronica's face. Her facial expressions and moans were turning him on even more. The wetter her pussy got, the more excited he got. It wasn't until he noticed her eyes rolling back that he pulled out of her.

"Turn over," he suggested, helping her off the desk.

Doggy style was her favorite position, and when he entered her from the back, she lost her breath. What made him enjoy it even more was the roundness and softness of her ass and the way it shook when he went in and out, causing her to run from his dick. His grip around her hips made that hard to do though. To make sure she didn't try to get away, he grabbed a handful of her hair.

"Yesssss, give it to me," Veronica moaned loudly.

His pace became so fast, that Veronica could only get one word out every few seconds, just trying to tell him how good his dick was, and occasionally saying it hurt so good. She felt herself trembling again and turned to look at him.

"I'm gonna cum all over this dick, daddy! I want you to cum with me! Cum inside of me, please. I want to feel it shoot all up inside of my pussy. Oh my fucking God, yes, just keep going."

That encouragement was all it took for Steven's body to tense up, and seconds later, both of them came simultaneously. Veronica felt his warm cum squirt inside of her and praised herself for getting exactly what she had come for. Her pussy would probably be sore for a couple of weeks, but it was well worth it.

"Damn, that was good," Steven said, out of breath.

He was more than satisfied as he slid his cum-covered dick out of her, slapped her on the ass, and then sat in the chair to catch his breath.

"That was fun," she replied, seductively rubbing her legs together.

"I'm glad you enjoyed it. I just have one request. Under no circumstances do you say anything to anybody. Do you understand what I'm saying to you?"

"Yes, I understand," she replied somewhat submissively. "But can we do this again soon?"

"I don't know, Veronica, I'm married," he said, putting on his clothes.

"Please?" she begged in a whiny voice.

"We'll see, okay? Let's get out of here before someone comes in and catches us. You know how gossipy people are in here."

They both left out of there with smiles on their faces. Veronica was surprised that she just had sex with her college professor. If they would have been caught, she would have gotten expelled and he fired. What excited her was the fact that they took that chance. She didn't mind doing something adventurous again as long as it was with him. She was obsessed with Steven Kessler, and nobody was going to get in the way of her happiness.

***

"I'm glad you like the place. Would you like to finalize the lease agreement? You can move in as soon as tomorrow if we get the paperwork done today," the realtor explained as they walked out of the apartment.

"I really love the place, but I wanted to take a look at a few other places closer to my job before making my final decision," Greg lied. "How about I give you a call in a couple of hours with my answer?"

He was in search of a place to stay because he was fed up with living with his parents. Ever since he moved out of the house he and Symira had been sharing, he had been staying in his old room. It was nothing like when he was a kid, because he had no privacy. His parents even looked at him differently after finding out he was HIV positive.

"Okay, let me know whatever you decide. If it's any consolation, I'll throw in a free month. It's up to you, but you have my number."

That offer was very enticing, and he had to take a moment to consider it. By the time he left there, not only did he have the apartment, but he also had talked the realtor into giving him an extra free month. He was a little suspicious at first about why she was trying so hard to rent the unit out, but he later found out that she had a quota to meet by the end of the week or else her brother was going to take the building away from her again.

***

"Where are you?"

"Why?"

"I need to pick up the rest of my stuff. Can I meet you at the house?" he asked.

"What time, 'cause I'm out taking care of some business." Symira asked. She really wasn't busy, she just didn't feel like being bothered with him right now.

"I'm on my way to handle some other things. How about I hit you up in about two hours?" Greg said as he turned onto the expressway, heading to his doctor's appointment.

"Fine, just call before you come, to make sure I'm there."

"Okay I—" he started to say, but she had disconnected the call already. "Bitch!"

He really hated everything about her now. The person he once had loved unconditionally, now was the one he wished would drop dead. It was her who cheated on him with her own boss, and it was because of her that he got infected with an incurable disease. His life was slowly fading, but it wasn't going to affect his way of living. He was determined to live life to the fullest until the day he was called home. He decided to go out and enjoy himself tonight after he picked up the rest of his stuff from his old house and got settled into his new apartment.

Symira and her friend were on their way to meet up with Morgan at his home in Harrisburg. He had called her and suggested that they meet. She told him she was bringing a friend and that they would be there by six that evening.

"What do you think he wants to meet you for, and why couldn't Mr. Governor come to see you instead of you having to go way out there?" Nancy asked with sarcasm in her voice.

"I guess he wants to talk about the arrangements I suggested. That's all I'm trying to hear right now. If he play games, I will just have to drop a lil birdie to the press."

"You are so bad," Nancy replied, reaching over and sticking her hand under Symira's dress. "Just like I thought, no panties."

"Stop, girl, you gonna make me crash," Symira responded, pushing her hand away.

"You know you like it," Nancy teased.

"I do, but business before pleasure, okay?"

"Okay!" she replied, patting Symira's leg.

"When we get out there, I want you to act subtle no matter what I say, 'cause I know how you are if someone says something crazy. Can you do that?" Symira asked as she turned onto I-81 toward Harrisburg, Pennsylvania.

Nancy gave her a dirty look, but knew her friend was right. She hated men that tried their best to take advantage of women. That was one of the reasons she didn't have a man in her life. She treated them like toys, and only used them as such.

"I got you," she said, applying more lip gloss on her lips.

Symira felt her stomach, thinking about how life for her child would be. All she ever wanted was a

family, but she couldn't have the person she pre-
ferred. When they arrived at Morgan's home, she
texted him letting him know she was there.

Morgan stepped out of the house wearing a wifebeater and a pair of shorts. He looked like he was
about to work out. Both women sat in the car admiring his body. Nancy had to squeeze her legs together
to avoid the juices that were beginning to ease out
into her panties.

"Damn, girl, he is fine," Nancy stated, looking at
the way his muscles fought to break out of his tank
top. "Why did y'all break up?"

"It's a long story that I prefer not to talk about at
this time," she said, grabbing her purse and exiting
the car.

When she stepped out, she gave Morgan a half
hug. He looked her over, admiring the dress she was
sporting. She looked as if she had just stepped off the
runway. When Nancy stepped out, Morgan's eyes
went straight to her ass, as she purposely bent over to
pick her cellphone up. First thing he thought about
was how good it would feel to be hitting her from the
back.

"Who is your friend?"

"Nancy, Morgan, Morgan, Nancy!"

"Nice to meet you, Mr. Governor," Nancy said, shaking his hand. She felt a bit of a spark between the two of them.

"Just call me Morgan. Right this way, ladies," he motioned, escorting them into his home.

"We can't stay long," Symira told him.

"Don't worry, I won't keep you too long. Would you like anything to drink, Nancy?" he asked, pouring himself a drink.

"Whatever you make, thank you."

"What kind of juice do you want, Symira, 'cause I know you're not drinking any liquor."

She just sucked her teeth and sat down. "I'm good. Can we discuss what I came here for?" she insisted, rubbing her stomach.

Morgan smiled, loving that she still was that feisty woman that came to his office years ago for a job. He wished things could have worked out differently, but she had him by the balls, and there was nothing he could do about it. They sat and talked for over an hour, with Morgan doing most of the listening instead of talking. After it was all said and done, he had agreed to most of her demands in order to keep his infidelity a secret from the press.

"So when will I get my money?"

"I'll send you a check first thing in the morning. Would you and your friend like to stay for dinner tonight? You can head back home in the morning. I really don't want you driving in all that traffic, because there was a really bad accident on I-81."

"I will ask Nancy and see what she wants to do," Symira said, walking out his office to see where her friend was.

Nancy was in the living room watching television. Symira sat next to her, and they talked for a couple of minutes, smiling at each other. They ended up agreeing with him, and he showed them to the guest rooms so they could relax before going out to dinner. Even though he had a security detail, he still frequently ditched them for a while, and tonight was going to be one of them.

***

That night, Symira, Nancy, and Morgan had a good time. He took them to dinner, and then they went to a Spanish club where they danced and had drinks until the wee hours of the morning. It was around three in the morning when they returned home.

"I'm so tired. I'm going to bed so I will be ready to drive in the morning," Symira said. "Nancy, which room do you want?"

"It doesn't matter. Goodnight, Morgan, and thanks for showing us a good time," Nancy replied as they headed toward the stairs.

"Symira, if that bed not comfortable, you can stay in my room," he suggested.

"I should be cool," she said, blowing his invitation off.

He watched them go upstairs and then walked over to his closet, changed into a pair of shorts, and went over to his bar and poured himself another drink before sitting on the couch. He clicked on the television and started watching a soft porn movie called *Zane Diaries*. He made sure no one was coming and then stuck his hand inside his shorts and gripped his manhood. As he watched the girl-on-girl scene, he stroked and stroked his dick until he heard a noise behind him. He quickly pulled his hand out of his shorts.

"Looks like someone is horny tonight," Nancy said with a slurred voice. She was tipsy and also horny. She had been watching him from the steps, and decided to join him.

"What about Symira?"

"She's out like a baby, so I guess we have to be quiet," she replied, sitting on his lap and kissing him passionately on the lips.

He gripped her ass and squeezed it as they began dry humping each other. Nancy pulled away and sat next to him on the couch. She only had on the T-shirt that he had given her and her panties. She lifted the shirt over her head, exposing her nice firm breasts.

"You want me to fuck you, don't you?"

She nodded as she moved a hand over her naked breast and made his way down her belly, rubbing her pussy lips through the fabric of her panties. Nancy was getting even wetter each time she touched herself.

"Come here," she moaned, pushing his head toward her pussy while her other hand peeled off her wet panties. "I want to see what you can do with that thick tongue of yours."

"As you wish," he replied.

Morgan went straight to work on her clit, flicking it with hard, fast tongue strokes, or at times sucking it between his lips. In no time her legs tensed up and she moaned loudly, flooded by an orgasm. He had to cover her mouth to muffle the sound. He moved between her legs and buried his dick in her. Morgan glided his shaft slowly in and out of her, but it was soon evident that she wanted it hard and fast. He gave her exactly what she wanted, pounding away at her moistness.

After they fucked for a few, Morgan felt his climax coming on. He rubbed her nipples while pumping faster and faster in and out of her. Nancy tensed up again, and he was on the brink of coming. Morgan shoved deep into her and let loose. She let out a howl as she released another orgasm. Her contractions seemed to milk twice the usual cum from his balls as they had their first simultaneous orgasm.

"Damn, that was good. Your ass is so fat, I need to hit that from behind," he declared.

"I see you're still ready," she answered, slowly turning around and sticking her ass in the air. Morgan grabbed her round ass and entered her doggy-style.

Nancy was gasping and moaning real loud as he fucked her harder.

"Oh shit, harder, harder," she screamed out, pushing her ass back to meet his thrust.

Morgan once again had to cover her mouth, hoping that Symira didn't hear their sexcapade that was taking place behind her back. He fondled her breasts and continued stroking away from behind until he felt his semen building up once again. Wanting it to last a little longer, he pulled out of her.

"Was that what you wanted?" was her immediate reply, thinking he was done.

"I'm not done with you yet," he shot back.

He pulled her to the floor and then entered her again, pulling her legs up to his shoulders. She felt like his rod was going to bust through her stomach the way he was deep stroking her. Morgan was oblivious to her screams now as he tried to reach his climax.

"I'm about to cum," he moaned, pumping even harder and faster.

"Cum inside me, baby. I want to feel your sperm dripping out of me."

That's all it took to drive him over the edge. Morgan grunted and then shot his load deep inside her pussy. He leaned down, and they started kissing.

"What the fuck is going on?"

Both Morgan and Nancy jumped at the sound of the voice. They looked up and found an angry Symira staring down at them. Her yellow complexion was now beet red. Morgan thought he saw steam coming from her body.

"Symira, it's not what you think," Nancy tried to say.

"Bitch, it's exactly what I think. I brought you here to support me, and now you're fucking my baby father. I should have never trusted you."

"Calm down, Symira, it's not that serious. You are overreacting to nothing, and—" he started to say, but was met with a blow to the face.

He was able to catch her next swing, and pushed her backward. Symira stumbled and fell through the coffee table. She screamed out in pain, holding her stomach. Blood was coming from her shirt in the area that would indicate her having a miscarriage.

"Oh my God," Nancy blurted out, jumping off the floor and rushing over to her friend.

"Agghhhh," Symira screamed out in pain.

Morgan called for an ambulance. Then he and Nancy quickly got dressed, waiting for it to arrive to help Symira. The ambulance rushed her to the hospital, but Morgan couldn't stay with her, because of the media. Four hours later the doctor hit them with the tragic news that she had lost the baby. He said the cause was stress and blunt force from the fall she took. Symira was heartbroken about the situation and placed all the blame on her best friend and Morgan. She knew her friend was a whore, but didn't expect her to stoop that low, especially when she knew how Symira felt about him. The only thing on her mind as she lay in that hospital bed was how she would make the both of them pay. Revenge weighed heavy in her heart.

SEVEN

EVERYONE WAS AT THE hospital visiting Michelle with Sasha as she recovered from her traumatic ordeal. They both already had spoken with detectives on more than one occasion about the whole abduction, and were relieved to know that it was over. Akiylah had stayed home because she had hurt her back earlier trying to pick up a heavy box in the garage. Her sister, Vanessa, went back to the Virgin Islands to be with her mom.

Sahmeer told Akiylah that his trainer would be there to look at her back when she left her office, so Akiylah decided to take a soothing bath while she waited. Her cell phone went off interrupting her relaxation time. When she looked to see who it was, her eyes lit up.

"Hello, baby, me miss you and so do me kitty," she softly said, sticking her hand in her pussy.

"Did you do what I asked you to do?"

"Yes, me took care of it today just like you said. Are you coming to see me tonight?"

"No, I have to go out to Delaware to meet with someone, but if I make it back tonight, we will have some fun," he replied.

"Okay, me love you!

"Me too!" he said before ending the call.

She finished bathing and playing with herself and then got out of the tub and dried off. She went into the bedroom to get dressed. After rubbing herself down with the Victoria Secret lotion, she put on a pair of boy shorts and a tank top. She started looking through one of the magazines that was on the nightstand.

"Akiylah, are you here?"

"Me upstairs," she yelled out to Lorena, letting her know where she was.

Seconds later, Lorena entered the room with her massage equipment. She set her table up and then pulled out the oils, amongst other things, and sat them beside the table. The whole-time Lorena was getting ready, Akiylah was replaying their last encounter in her head. Thoughts of how she touched her made her start to shiver in anticipation.

"Are you ready, ma'am?"

"Yes!" Akiylah replied, lying on the table. "Okay, what do you want me to do?"

"Just relax while I put on some music," Lorena said, turning on the stereo. "You can keep your shorts on. You have to remove your shirt."

Lorena lit up the savory scented incense and dimmed the lighting. As the soft music played, she directed Akiylah to lie on her back. After pouring some of the massage oil into her palms, she rubbed her hands together to warm the oil up and kneaded it into Akiylah's soft neck and shoulders. Akiylah was getting hot, so she voluntarily removed her shorts and tossed them on the bed.

"This is just what me needed," she moaned in her native accent.

Lorena squeezed out some more of the oil and applied it to Akiylah's pubic area. She rubbed it onto her snatch and then slipped a finger into her moist, warm hole, as moans of ecstasy escaped her lips. After a few moments, she eased her finger out and proceeded to knead the scented oil into her lower torso, legs, calves, and feet.

At that point, Lorena asked Akiylah to turn over so she could rub some oil on her shoulders and back. Lorena nearly drooled at the sight of the nice fat caramel ass that laid before her. Using more than enough oil, she rubbed it slowly into those round cheeks, marveling at their baby-soft texture.

"Mmmmmmmm, don't stop!"

She poured an enormous amount of the oil between Akiylah's cheeks. She watched as it slowly ran down over Akiylah's puckered asshole and in between her legs. Lorena caught as much of the oil as she could on her fingers, and then slowly eased one of them into Akiylah's asshole.

"Ohhh," a moan of delight escaped Akiylah's lips as Lorena's finger slid deeper and deeper. "Me love the way your hand feels."

"Shhhhh, just let me take care of you," Lorena answered.

As Lorena fingered her asshole, Akiylah humped her finger lustfully, meeting it thrust for thrust, squeezing her cheeks and pumping at the same time.

"Put it in me pussy, baby."

Lorena quickly obliged, planting two fingers into her hungry pussy, sending her into a trembling climax. Akiylah shook from head to toe as waves of pleasure coursed through her body. She lay there spent from what just happened, but Lorena wasn't done with her yet. She spread her legs wider than they had been and buried her face in Akiylah's already wet and trembling pussy.

"Oh, me God, please, I had enough," she purposefully whined, feeling another orgasm fast approaching.

"Cum in my mouth," Lorena softly said, and then stuck a finger in her ass for added effect.

That drove Akiylah over the edge as her juices flushed out into Lorena's mouth. She swallowed every drop of it. She then walked over and kissed Akiylah, letting her taste her own secretions. The two of them had another session together before Lorena had to leave. Akiykah was still horny after all they'd just got finished doing. She walked into Sasha's room and looked in her drawer until she found what she was looking for. She then headed back to her own room and went to work on herself with one of

Sasha's dildos, until she relieved herself two more times.

***

Raphael and Carla were leaving from the opera house after enjoying a wonderful show. They decided to stop and get something to eat at the Red Lobster on City Line Avenue. The place was so packed that they were told it would be about an hour wait. They sat in the waiting area until they were called to their seats.

"Excuse me, are you the one that is married to the governor?" a pedestrian asked.

"Yes, I was, how can I help you?" Carla replied in a polite manner.

"That wasn't you that was just on the news? I came over to say sorry for your loss, but I guess I had the wrong person."

"Wait, what are you talking about? I wasn't in no hospital," Carla said, now piqued by this sudden revelation.

"I'm talking about this!"

The lady pulled out her iPhone and showed her the story line that was breaking news on every social media network. Sure enough, it was Morgan outside of the hospital, and they were asking him about his wife losing their baby. He wasn't expecting the media to be there as he tried to leave, but to his surprise they were. His security team pushed through the crowd and helped him inside one of the awaiting SUVs.

"Who is the person they're talking about?"

"Symira!"

At the sound of that name, Carla's whole reaction changed. She passed the girl back her phone and walked outside. Raphael followed behind her to make sure she was okay. He knew almost everything about her previous life, even how Morgan had cheated on her. He never wanted to see her hurting again, and promised to keep her happy.

"Are you okay, Carla?" he asked, opening the car door for her.

"I'll be fine. I just want to go home."

They headed home without saying a word. Carla was in deep thought about the baby he was about to have with his tramp secretary. What had her so jealous was the fact that she couldn't get pregnant because she kept having miscarriages. Raphael couldn't help but wonder if their relationship was going to take a beating because of what had happened. He just hoped that she would still love him like he loved her.

***

Kevin's funeral was packed to capacity with family, friends, fans, and paparazzi. Security was so tight that if you weren't somebody, you weren't getting in. There were many players that came out to show their support for Kevin's family. Michelle made sure that he had an open casket so everyone could see his handsome face. She really had a hidden agenda no one knew about.

"We are gathered here today to say goodbye to one of the most well-respected men in not only our city but also our hearts," the pastor of the church began.

Everyone in the church had tears in their eyes as they listened to him give the eulogy. Michelle Michael, Sasha, Marcus, and Sahmeer all sat together in the front row. Akiylah and a couple other close relatives sat behind them. The whole service lasted around three hours, and then they headed to the burial ground to lay him down for good. Michelle's performance could have definitely won her an Oscar. If everyone only had known the logistics of the situation, they would have thrown her in that hole with him.

They were now at the repast, and that was also packed to capacity. Sasha had rented out the community center thanks to Carla and Raphael. They had also attended the funeral, but stayed in the background because of everything that was going on in their own lives.

"Thank you so much for setting all this up for us. The whole setup is really nice."

"I'm just sorry for your loss, and I hope that everything that happened to you and your family will somehow turn into a positive instead of a negative," Carla said, pouring herself a drink.

"Well, time heals all wounds, and I know that he will always be me and Michael's angel," Michelle replied. "My only concern is making sure that he is okay. I have been gone for a while and never thought that I would see any of them again. My son really has been taking this the hardest, and I have to be there for him 'cause he will need me more than ever right now."

"You can't ever forget about what happened to you, Michelle. That was a very disturbing chain of events, and it's going to take some time to resolve."

"I know. I'm just tired, so once again, thank you for everything," Michelle said, giving Carla a hug before walking off.

Michelle left out of there because she was tired of being fake. It was time to put her plan in motion. She wanted to get rid of all the fake people in her life that deceived her in some kind of way. Sasha was the next person on her list because she was one of the biggest threats to her.

"Hey, I'm on my way to see you. Something went wrong, and you may be hearing about it real soon," she said, speaking into her cell phone.

"You know where I'm at. Just make sure you're not followed."

"Why would I be—?"

"Just taking precautions," he cut her off.

"See you soon," she replied, disconnecting the call.

EIGHT

"THERE'S SOMETHING ABOUT THIS whole story that's just not adding up if you ask me," Det. Hill said looking over the Green case.

"Well, let's hear your theory," her partner said.

"When we interviewed Michelle the first time, she said that they had held her prisoner in an apartment somewhere, but didn't know where. The second time we interviewed her, she said the basement."

"Okay, wait a minute, when we found them, they were in the basement. What are you trying to say?" Det. Jones asked, trying to get to the bottom of the whole thing.

"I'm saying there's more to this story, and before I can close this case, we may need to do some additional investigating."

"The boss is never gonna go for that unless you have some solid proof. The first thing he is going to say because of the publicity is, we need to wrap it up because the higher ups are watching and want someone to pay. Since the culprits are dead, they most likely will say that it's over."

"I don't think that was everybody involved. Just trust me on this, okay? Let's go over all the evidence again, and if you're not convinced that something's not right, I'll be the first one to sign off on the paperwork to close it."

"Okay, partner, where do we start?" she said, sitting down at her desk.

"Well first let's go over each statement and highlight anything that stands out. Then we'll go over the evidence we collected. There has to be something we're overlooking."

"I'll start with these right here while you're going through that," she said, picking up three folders off the desk.

Cynthia grabbed the other stuff and started examining it. Her phone started ringing, and when she answered it, her whole facial expression changed. She hung up and then looked at her partner.

"Grab your stuff. That was the forensics team. They want to see us ASAP about the evidence we dropped off."

"Did they say what they found?" she asked as they rushed out of the station.

"We'll know in a few minutes," Cynthia replied.

It only took them about fifteen minutes to get to the forensics lab, because they lit it up the whole way. They headed straight to the office to find out what was so important. After flashing their badges, they waited to hear from their expert.

"Cynthia, Theresa, it's nice to see you," Arnold started. "I have some interesting news for you, and I think it will answer the questions you've been inquiring about."

"What is it?" Cynthia asked anxiously.

"Well, you were right, there were more people involved than originally suspected. We have two other fingerprints that weren't in the building. Here are the names that they came back to," he stated, passing the file to Cynthia.

She immediately recognized one of the assailants. She showed the file to her partner, and they both looked at each other and shook their heads.

"He has a criminal record that's longer than my arm," Theresa told her partner. "I see attempted murder, aggravated assault, grand theft, gun charges, and the list goes on and on."

"I arrested that asshole more than once about a year ago, and somehow the charges got dropped both times. You mean to tell me that he had something to do with the kidnapping and murder of that NBA player?"

"That's what the evidence is saying. There is something else though," he said, getting back to what he was saying. "I found this to be suspicious."

"What?"

"I found semen on Mr. Green's clothing, and when I checked the DNA, it wasn't his."

"So whose is it?" Theresa said, starting to get impatient.

"I don't know yet. We are trying to match it with the blood samples we collected from the scene. As soon as we know, I will personally call your cell phone."

"Is there anything else?"

"There is one more thing, and this is why I wanted to tell you in person," he stated, being serious.

"I'm listening!"

"I have reason to believe that this whole situation goes higher than our pay grades."

"What do you mean?" Cynthia replied.

"I have to show you instead, so you can tell me if I'm tripping or not," he stated, passing her another folder. "Before we are hired, we all have to give a blood sample just in case something ever happens to us and we can't be identified right away. Well, look whose blood was at the crime scene. At first I thought it was impossible, so I tested it again to make sure. It came back the same, so I called you immediately."

"Let me see that?" Theresa asked, looking over Cynthia's shoulder.

"Umm, can you grab that folder I left in the car? I want to see if he can tell us what he thinks it is," she said, not wanting her partner to see what she had just read.

"Okay, I'll be right back," she replied, exiting the room without any protest.

They both read the file again in disbelief while the forensic specialist continued explaining his new findings. Cynthia was speechless. He went over every detail with her, leaving out not a single detail. Cynthia was so surprised about the newfound information that she had to sit down. She was wondering how the hell this had gotten so bad.

"Who else knows about this?" she asked him.

"You're the first person, but I have to give this to my captain so he can contact the brass. This is really bad, Detective."

Cynthia could not let this information get out. She had to think of something, and quick, so she played off the fact that he been wanting to fuck her since he first saw her.

"No, how about you let me drop it off to brass myself and you meet me as soon as you get off of work so you can finally get what you been asking for," she said, getting so close to him that he got nervous.

She had him right where she wanted him and then leaned in, giving him a kiss while grabbing his manhood. He felt like he was in heaven from her touch.

"Ohhh my, I get off at seven. Where can we meet at?" he said, forgetting about the importance of the folder that she now had in her possession.

"How about the Blue Moon on 51st and Westminster?" she whispered in his ear.

"I'll be there," he said, watching her walk toward the door. "Don't forget to drop that off. We have a crooked cop amongst us that has to be dealt with."

"I'll take care of it. You just don't have me waiting too long for you," she replied, blowing him a kiss and then leaving.

Cynthia had just made it out before her partner returned. She caught her just as she was getting off the elevator.

"I got the envelope," she said, passing it to Cynthia.

"An emergency came up, so he had to go to another crime scene. I told him that we would drop by tomorrow. Here, take the car back," Cynthia said, passing her partner the keys. "I'm going to head home for the night. I have something to take care of."

"You sure you don't need a ride?"

"No, I can take the subway. I'll see you tomorrow at work," Cynthia told her, walking toward Market Street.

"What happened with that folder you were looking at?"

"He's gonna make sure everything is correct and then give one of us a call. Make sure you keep your phone on," she said, leaving Theresa standing there.

Theresa found it very strange that as soon as Cynthia read whatever was inside that folder, she started acting so different and her whole demeanor changed. She brushed it off though because she didn't want to question a senior officer. Theresa got in the unmarked car and headed back to the station.

***

Arnold arrived at the motel a few minutes before Cynthia and sat in his car listening to music. He received a text message saying to come up to room 204 and get ready for a surprise. Arnold got out in a hurry and rushed up to the room. He walked into the dark room ready to finally have sex with his crush.

"Lay down on the bed and take off your clothes!" a voice whispered.

Arnold quickly stripped out of his clothes and jumped on the bed waiting to finally get laid by his coworker. He felt a pair of hands rubbing his rod, that was already at full attention. Then she cuffed him to the bed rails.

"Oh, so you like to be the dominant one, huh? Take me, baby, I'm all yours."

She climbed on top of him, slowly grinding her pussy lips up and down his shaft. Then she let his manhood slide deep into her hole. He wanted to grab her, but he was tied up and couldn't move. She was riding him like a wild woman, jumping up and down, sticking her nails into his skin.

"That's right, ride this dick," he moaned, feeling himself about to cum.

Before he could reach his climax, the door popped open. A man walked in holding a gun in his hand. Before either of them could scream, two bullets pierced their hearts. For good measure, the assailant put another round in both of their heads and then closed the door leaving a gruesome sight for whoever opened that room.

When the desk person heard the shots, she ducked behind the counter and called the police. It took them less than five minutes to arrive, but it was too late. The assailant was long gone. They searched almost every room on the second floor trying to find out if anyone was injured. They were just about to go to the third floor, when they stumbled across an opened door with a funny smell. What they saw when they went inside made their stomachs turn.

There were two naked bodies sprawled out across the bed, with multiple gunshot wounds. They declared that whole building a crime scene. No one was allowed in or out until detectives were able to interview them. Once they realized one of the victims was one of their own, they shut that whole side of West Philly down. Now they were looking for a cop killer.

"I don't care what it takes. Find the person that did this," the captain yelled at all of his detectives.

"You heard the man. Find that bastard and put him in a cage," their lieutenant said. "Theresa, where the hell is your partner?"

"I just texted her, sir. Waiting for her to get here now," she answered, looking at her phone to see if she had texted back yet.

"I need something to go with before the commissioner and mayor get here, so keep me informed," he demanded.

***

"I took care of that problem for you. This is the second time I watched your back. When are, you going to do the same for me?"

"I made you a lieutenant, but you weren't satisfied with that because you missed the streets. Now you want me to promote you again. Come on with the bullshit, Cynthia."

"I told you that I wanted my captain pins, and until then, you owe me, not the other way around," she informed him.

"We are on our way to that mess that you left. Be there by the time we get there," he said, ending the call before she had anything else to say.

Cynthia had been doing so much to help Pete since he became the DC. When she saw that it was some of his blood left at that hideout, she had no choice but to order the hit on Arnold, or he would have put Pete in a compromising predicament. She arrived on the scene, and Theresa hurried over to her car.

"Where have you been? The boss is going crazy over this."

"I tried getting here as fast as I could. What do we have?" Cynthia said, heading past the news reporters and inside the motel, with Theresa right on her heels, filling her in on the events.

"Both of them were hit at close range, once in their head and once in the chest."

"What in the hell was a cop doing in a dump like this?"

"You need to ask that question?" Theresa said, pointing to the hooker lying dead next to him. Cynthia knew why the hooker was there; after all, she was the one who had paid her. Now she had to clean up the loose ends.

"So, what can you tell me about this?" Pete stated, walking into the room.

"From our preliminary findings, it seems as if he came here with the lady. Then sometime while they were having sex, someone entered their room and murdered both of them. There was no forced entry and no signs of a struggle. We have people searching for any kind of fingerprints, but so far we have nothing."

"You know whoever it was, they wore gloves, so there will be no prints. I saw cameras when I came in. How about surveillance?" Pete asked.

"The manager said they have been broken for the last week so they don't know who's coming or going and can't even remember who they saw in the past two hours," Theresa chimed in because that was the first thing she checked on when she arrived.

"The back door was propped open when one of the officers checked, indicating whoever did this used it as their escape route," one of the other detectives mentioned.

Cynthia listened to everything that was being said and knew that the person she hired did a good job of being inconspicuous. However, she was not trying to leave any stones unturned. She knew what she had to do.

"I have to go deliver the news to his family with some of the other brass. Detective Hill, let me speak to you outside," Pete told her as an order, not a request.

"Let me know what you find out. I have to go get chewed out right now," she playfully said to her partner.

"I'll call you when I find out anything."

Cynthia stepped out of the motel, looking for her boss and former partner. When she spotted, him sitting in the backseat of his SUV, she walked over and hopped in. Pete rolled his window up before speaking.

"Thank you for taking care of that problem. Look, I know it feels like I've been different since taking on this new position, but I'm still your friend and will do whatever I can for you. All you had to do was keep that lieutenant job until I was able to assign you a captain position."

"I just wanted to be out and about."

"You could have done that as lieutenant too," he pointed out in disbelief. "What do you think you will be doing once you become captain of a precinct? I'll tell you: sitting at a damn desk. You blew a perfect opportunity to have as much control needed to operate with limited people on your back. What I need you to do now is put on your big-girl panties and step up to the plate."

"You're right, and I will stop being selfish. Anyway, I will be taking care of that other thing too so nothing falls back on us if anything ever takes a turn for the worst."

"Make it look like he resisted and had to be fatally subdued."

"Yes, sir," she smirked, stepping out the car.

As Cynthia drove home, she thought about all the things she had done in the past and how they affected her life now. She was once an outstanding police officer that followed all the rules. Now she was one of the crooked ones. She blamed it on her falling for a very beautiful woman who ended up getting killed during a robbery. She made up her mind that this would be her last criminal act, or so she thought.

NINE

IT HAD BEEN REALLY hard for Michael lately. First he lost his mother, and then when he found out that she was never dead, he lost his father. Those types of things can drive a sane man crazy. Akiylah saw how it was affecting him and wanted to do something to take his mind off of it. She lied to her husband and told him that she was going back to the islands to visit her mom, so that she could spend the weekend with Michael. He didn't know what was going on, when he received a text message saying that it was important to meet her. She gave him the address to a lodge out in New York, and he told her he would be there around ten.

Michael stopped at the reception desk to pick up the key to the lodge that he was instructed to go to, then walked over to it. When he opened the door, Akiylah was lying across the bed in a red and black thong set, motioning for him to come in. She had a pink vibrator in her hand, and she flicked on the switch. It began to hum softly as she stroked it across her titties, sighing at the buzzing touch. Her nipples quivered and stiffened even more.

"Mmmmmmmm, yes," she moaned, making the tip draw circles on her skin around her erect nipple. "Oooohhh, you like?"

Michael stood there watching her please herself. He locked the door, removed every article of clothing he had on, and got on the bed next to her. He continued to watch while stroking his own dick.

"You are such a fucking whore, and I like it."

She held the vibrator over her titties, enjoying the sensation. When she squeezed her thighs together, the juices oozed from her pussy like liquid from a sliced grapefruit. She moved the vibrator tip down her stomach, into her soaked hole. It touched her clit, and she almost came on the spot. Her eyes closed, and her head jerked back as her blood raced through her body.

"Yeeessss, that feels so good. Me want to cum again."

Akiylah moved the tip lower, to her itchy, wet pussy lips. She slid the vibrator along the crack, stroking the lips, allowing the point to ease carefully into her wet hole once again. Her pussy seemed to melt around the steadily buzzing plastic, as if she were turning into Jell-O.

"Wow!" Michael exclaimed as he watched her juices ease out every time the vibrator exited her insides.

Akiylah opened her eyes. He was still stroking his rod, and there was no question that he was enjoying the show. She continued to tease him for her own enjoyment.

"You look so slutty," he said in admiration. "I think I want some of that good pussy now."

"Really?" she moaned, moving the vibrator downward to her ass. "Oooohhhh!"

She squealed as the tip touched her opening and gave her a zingy thrill. It had no trouble spreading her ass muscles and easing into the lower end of her hole.

"Oh, fucking shittt!" she blurted out, working it against her asshole.

She took turns switching it from her ass to her pussy, teasing them provocatively with the battery-charged sex toy. She inserted two fingers into her ass while the vibrator played sexily with her pussy lips, making shallow penetrations and then sliding up to tickle her clit.

"I want to fuck you," Michael gasped, his hands and lips attacking her titties, not wanting to watch any longer.

Akiylah could feel his hard dick banging against her thigh as he licked her nipples. She was now anticipating his dick relieving the vibrator of its duties.

"Okay, baby," she giggled. "I want you to fuck me in the ass too. You fuck me there, and I will keep me fingers busy in me pussy, okay?"

"Why are you so kinky all of a sudden?" he asked. "I like this side of you."

"Me just wanted to give you something special," she said, happy to comply.

His dick didn't seem to mind if she was kinky, and if his stiffness was any indication, he was more than happy to serve some good, long deep strokes.

"Come here. I got just what you need."

Akiylah put pillows under her belly to lift her ass high. Michael got behind her, running his hands over her ass cheeks, testing her tight asshole with his fingers. She loved having anal sex. Ever since she learned she could cum like a river with something reaming out her tiny tight ass, she wanted to explore that newfound aspect of her sexuality. He was going to love it too.

"Let me get this first," she said, reaching behind her and stroking his penis, making sure it was fully erect.

She then grabbed the tube of lube off the nightstand and squirted some between her ass cheeks. She nibbled on her bottom lip in hungry expectation as Michael fondled her ass, spreading her cheeks wide to see her tiny well-lubed hole. His fingers began playing with the tight aperture as he got her ready for the real thing.

"Oh wow, your fingers feel so good," she moaned, as they moved inside her ass.

Then came the thrilling moment as his fingers plunged inside. She wanted to scream out in pleasure and pain. Akiylah thought it would be so much better when it was his dick and not just his fingers in there. She hungered for the explosion of his cum shooting inside her.

"You're so tight and greasy," he said. "Your butt is sucking my fingers in. You really want this, don't you? I think it's time to give it to you."

"Don't tell me, show me!" she moaned. "I know it's ready. I can feel it hitting against me hip. Take that big dick and shove it into me asshole now, baby, please," she begged.

Michael removed his fingers, making her moan louder. Then seconds later she felt the pressure of his hard dick ready to take its place. He pulled on her ass cheeks, spreading them as far apart as they would go. He then opened her ass splendidly with his finger. By now she was so turned on that her body was twitching.

"Put it in and fuck me please!" she urged.

"Don't rush me! Here it comes. Can you feel it, baby?" he stated.

"Oh fuck, can me ever!" Akiylah sighed, feeling his hard dick rubbing up and down her slit, then penetrating her. "Yes, it's going inside. Push harder . . . me want it all, yessssssss."

She screamed as he slid all the way up in her until his belly ground against her quivering body. It felt so good that she couldn't even speak.

"Oh yes, now go faster and harder. Me can take it. I'm so horny, baby," she screamed.

Michael began to speed up the pace. The lube made it so loose and wet that his dick kept sliding out. He kept a steady pace, each stroke slamming deep into Akiylah's guts, and her screams were shrill as the pleasure became almost too much to bear.

"Me about to cum. Fuck me harder," she said, feeling her orgasm building up.

Moments later she did, lurching under him, bucking like a horse, her body gone wild with hot release. He too was almost there. She could feel it in the savage intensity with which he stabbed her, and could hear it in the way he moaned and sighed as he forced himself to a couple more pumps before letting go.

"I'm cummmmmmming!" he screamed, releasing his own semen deep inside Akilyah's shaking body. They both fell onto the bed.

They lay there until they heard the sound of someone else coming in. Michael was ready to jump up, but Akiylah stopped him.

"Shhhhhhh, me have another surprise for you."

Ten seconds later, Lorena walked into the room wearing nothing but a jacket to cover up her nakedness. She let it fall to the floor, and then she eased over to bed, crawling in between the two of them.

"Mind if I join in?" she seductively moaned, rubbing Michael's inner thighs.

"Surprise, honey! This is for you," Akiylah said excitedly.

"Fuck yeah. Let the games begin," he replied, squeezing one of Lorena's firm breasts.

He knew who she was because every time she came to help Sahmeer with his therapy, he would watch the way her ass would move as she bent down for the different massage oils.

"Somebody's happy to see me," Lorena replied, looking at his erection.

Akiylah moved over to one of the chairs to watch the action that was about to unfold. She heard the slurping noises as Lorena took Michael's penis into her mouth and performed her best blow job performance.

"Let me taste you," he said, flipping her on her back and diving in head first between her legs. His tongue was like a snake as it made circles around her clit. She grabbed his head, pushing it deeper between her legs. He was sending her body into a frenzy. Akiylah felt herself getting horny all over again, and began playing with her pussy. Michael moved up Lorena's body and entered her without even thinking to use protection. Lorena was thumping her fist on the front of the headrest.

"Fuck me! Ooohh yes, fuck me. It feels so fucking good."

They switched positions with Lorena on top, back to front. He filled his hands with her sumptuous breasts, mauling her plush mounds while she did a little fandango with her pussy, above and upon the pointing tip of his hot and hard dick. She held him in one hand, spread her pussy lips with the other, and slid down on his rod.

"Damn, you are so fucking wet," he whispered as she bounced up and down on his shaft. It felt so good to both of them.

There was no question that she was ready for this moment, and her pussy seemed to beg for the continuous pounding it was taking.

"Oh shit, Michael! I'm fucking loving this, baby! Keep fucking me, just like that." She smiled, looking down as his dick appeared and then disappeared inside her hot walls.

Lorena rode her pussy down onto the upward thrust of his dick, and they humped hotly together, grinding, and swaying rhythmically. Akiylah couldn't keep her hands still. Her clit itched, and it seemed to have swollen up as if a bee had stung her right on the love button. Her fingers found her spot and attacked it savagely as she watched Michael fucking Lorena ferociously.

"I feel it coming again," Lorena moaned, moving faster.

Feeling her pussy contracting spasmodically around his dick, Michael gave her clit a wicked rub, causing her to lose control. He continued to caress it until she climaxed.

"Yessss, oooohhhh, squeeze it. I'm going to shoot my cum out of it and get your hand all white and sticky. Here it comes, baby. Oh shitttttt," she screamed, convulsing on his hand and dick.

Michael just kept on fucking in and out of her, spreading her leaking pussy lips almost to the breaking point, making more and more friction in her clit area.

"I'm about to bust my load," he grunted.

"Cum on my belly!" she gasped. "Not inside me, okay?"

"You got it," he grunted once again, and before he could get another word out, he pulled out, squirting his semen all over her.

Lorena reached down, scooping up the puddly glops of cum that lay warm and sticky on her body. She looked at Akiylah, who was reaching another orgasm of her own, and wiped her cum-soaked hand across her lips and licked Michael's semen off her sticky fingers.

"That really tastes good. Are we done, or do you have something else for me?" Lorena asked.

"Well, that all depends on how fast you can get me back up."

"That shouldn't be a problem," Akiylah replied, coming over to help Lorena with the task at hand.

They continued their little sexcapade for the whole weekend with threesome after threesome. By the time Michael went home on Sunday, he was burnt out and so were the ladies. It definitely was a mission complete for Akiylah. Now she had to get rid of Sahmeer so she could have Michael all to herself. She was about to find out that it would be easier said than done.

TEN

DEVON STEPPED IN HOAGIE City to grab a couple Dutches before heading home for the night. He had just left the strip club and was supposed to meet up with one of his many women at her spot-on Melon Street. When he walked up to the counter, he noticed that there was another customer waiting for her food. She had on a one-piece body suit that was so tight you could see her camel toe poking out. He walked up behind her and touched her on the shoulder.

"What's up with you? Why are you out here this time of night?" he asked, trying to pay for both of their meals.

She turned around and gave him a smile before saying, "My husband!" Then she flashed her wedding ring in his direction.

"Oh, I apologize!" he said, looking at the humongous rock on her finger.

"It's okay, you didn't know."

He politely backed up off of her. She thanked him for paying for her food and then headed for the door. Devon grabbed his stuff and followed her out.

"He is a very lucky man," he commented, watching her walk toward her car. She gave him an extra thrust of the hips, just to tease him.

"I know, he sure is," she politely said, before getting in the car and pulling off.

Devon got in his own car and pulled off, heading over to Melon Street. As soon as he turned onto 39th Street, he noticed lights flashing behind him. He knew he hadn't done anything wrong, so he was wondering why was he being pulled over. He stopped and reached into the glove compartment to retrieve his paperwork. The officer stepped out of the car and then approached the driver's side of the vehicle, with her hand not too far from her weapon.

"What did I do, officer? I was just on my way to a friend's house for the night. Here is all of my paperwork, and my license," he said, reaching into his back pocket.

"That won't be necessary," the officer replied, just before sticking a knife through his neck.

"Ugghhh," he screamed out, reaching for his neck.

"Sorry about this! I can't have you saying anything if you get caught."

She repeatedly pulled it out and stuck it back in three more times to make sure he wouldn't walk out of there alive. Devon kept gasping for air until he could no longer fight it. He died within seconds of the third puncture. Cynthia looked around to make sure nobody had witnessed what she just did. She then wiped the knife off on his shirt. She rushed back to her car and pulled off. She had just killed the link to her involvement in the kidnapping and murder of Kevin. This time she had made a mistake, because unbeknownst to her, a couple of kids were sitting outside their house smoking weed when she committed the murder. One of them even recorded her running back to her car and pulling off. She would soon find out that not listening to Pete would prove costly for her and anyone involved.

***

"The cause of death was multiple stab wounds to the neck," the coroner explained as he examined the body.

"His wallet is right here in his pocket," Theresa replied, removing it from his pants.

When she read the address, something immediately stood out to her. Then it suddenly hit her where she recognized it from. It was the same address from one of the cases they were working. The house that the basketball player was murdered in.

"Cynthia, something's not right here. The vic's address matches the address where we found that basketball player and his neighbor. We may have just stumbled across our suspects."

"So, somebody beat us to the punch," Cynthia replied.

"I guess so! What is the connection though? We may need to talk to Mrs. Green again to see if there was anything she left out."

"She told us everything she knew, and the lady is still grieving the loss of her husband. Let's just close this case and be done with it, okay?"

"Not so fast, partner. We have to find out who murdered him."

"Look where we are, Theresa. He probably came down here to cop something or who knows what. Maybe he even tried to burn them."

"That's why it's our job to find out. We are homicide detectives, right?" Theresa stated with a lot of sarcasm in her voice.

Cynthia picked right up on it and was about to respond to her, but an officer walked up on them scribbling on the pad he had in his hand.

"Excuse me, Detectives, I think we have something."

"What is it?" Theresa asked.

"I have a witness that said he saw a cop in plain clothes pulling away from that car."

"What are you talking about?" Cynthia chimed in. She started getting nervous. She had used an unmarked police car to commit a murder. Luckily it didn't have a camera on it.

"He said she was in a regular car and it had sirens and lights," the officer said, reading from his pad. "He also told me that she was in a hurry."

"Where is this witness at now?"

"He's standing over there," the officer replied, pointing toward the group of kids standing behind the crime scene tape. "He was scared to say anything because he and his friends were smoking marijuana in front of that building over there."

"So how the hell we suppose to believe some pothead," Cynthia blurted out.

"Because of this!"

The officer handed a cellphone over to Theresa. Cynthia looked like she had just seen a ghost. If her partner would have seen her face, she would have known how guilty she looked.

"He said it shows a female, but you can't see the face. I haven't looked at it. I just brought it straight to you."

"Good job, officer! I will get our team to pull the footage off of this and get it back to him by tomorrow."

"Let me take a look at that? Maybe we can figure out who it is on there," Cynthia said, reaching for the phone. She knew that phone was the key to her sitting behind bars for the rest of her life or not.

"We can watch it together."

"No, I need you to finish taking care of this. I will meet you back at the station," Cynthia replied, taking the phone from Theresa.

"I thought we were partners."

"We are. That's why I will handle this, and you handle that," she smirked, walking away.

Theresa just shook her head in defeat and headed over to finish securing the scene. Cynthia got into her car and leaned her head back on the headrest. She took a deep breath, feeling relieved that she had her hands on the only piece of evidence that could link her to that murder. She was a very good detective that should have never put herself in that kind of predicament, but she had, and now it was time to destroy it. She sat in the car watching the video, shaking her head in disgrace of what she was seeing. A rookie cop would have been able to pick her out of that footage. She pressed delete, put the phone in an evidence bag, and then headed back to the station.

***

Theresa returned to work the next day, ready to get the police impersonator that had committed this heinous crime. Cynthia was already there in the captain's office when she arrived. Theresa poured some coffee and then joined them.

"I tried calling you last night, but your phone went straight to voicemail," Theresa said to her partner, passing her a cup.

"Thank you, but we have a problem: there wasn't any video on that phone. I just had an officer return the phone to the kid."

"That's not right! He told us that it was. Why would he lie?"

"I checked it also, and there wasn't anything there," the captain replied.

Theresa really wasn't buying the story her partner was telling her, but she had to believe her boss. She left the office and decided to swing past the area where the kids were to see if she could find out what was going on. She knew there was something going on with her partner, but what?

She turned onto 39th Street in search of the kid that was trying to be helpful. When she spotted him and his friends, she pulled over and hopped out. The group of kids started stamping out the marijuana when they saw her badge.

"Don't be alarmed. I'm not here to arrest anybody. I just want to speak with the person that had his phone taken last night by one of my officers."

She made sure his friends wouldn't think he was a snitch. That was the last thing she wanted to do to someone that tried to do the right thing. The kid picked up on her vibe and played along.

"Your pig friends deleted my pictures and then gave me my phone back talking about they didn't touch it. What y'all trying to cover up the fact that there's a dirty cop on the force?"

"I need you to come to the station to get reimbursed for the damage they cost you."

"How do I know you're not trying to shut me up?" he replied, walking toward her. He gave her a wink and then headed up the street. "I'm out of here!"

Theresa got back in her car and then drove around the block to catch up with the kid. She spotted him standing by a car and pulled up on him. He got in the backseat, and she headed back to the station.

"Are you sure the person in that video was a cop?"

"I know what I saw, 'cause I wanted to put it on social media, but that cop asked can he show some detectives."

"Did you save it to the cloud or anything?" she asked.

"No!"

"Well, I want you to tell me and my partner what you saw, and if you could give us any details, that would help so much," she said, pulling into a parking spot.

They walked into the station, and soon as he spotted Cynthia, he stopped in mid-stride. He suddenly realized that that was the person he had seen fleeing from the scene.

"That's her," he whispered.

"What you say?" Theresa replied, turning to see who he was talking about.

"That's her right there," he said again, pointing at Cynthia.

"Are you sure?"

"I'm positive! That is the cop I saw jumping back in the car. She was there!"

"Okay, come with me. I have to get you out of here," she said, pulling him back out of the police station.

She knew something was up with her partner, but now it was confirmed. She just didn't know how a decorated officer was caught up in something like this. Theresa and the kid left the station, and she took him back home.

"I don't want you saying anything to anybody until I figure out what is going on. You are a very brave young man. Here is my number just in case you need to contact me for anything," she told him, passing him her card.

"Why don't you lock her up. You are a cop, right?"

"It's not that simple! I'm going to talk to my lieutenant, and we will get her. Don't worry, okay?" she said, pulling off.

Theresa headed back to give the disturbing news about her partner to her lieutenant. When she first became a cop, she thought she could help clean up the streets from the dealers and anyone else breaking the law. Never did she think she would have to take one of her own down. She hated dirty cops, and to find out it was her own partner disturbed her even more. She hoped like hell no one else knew about this.

***

"This is very disturbing news. Who else knows about this?" Theresa's lieutenant asked as he processed the news he was just given.

"I came to you first, sir. I thought you should know before I talk to Internal Affairs."

"Where is the kid that identified her?"

"I took him back and told him not to say anything until he heard from me. He doesn't trust the police right now, and you can see why." She shrugged.

"Okay, get your piece of shit partner in here, and you take the rest of the day off. I'll take care of this. I need a full statement from him also. I expect it on my desk by tomorrow."

"Yes, sir!" she replied.

Theresa left his office and went back to her desk. Cynthia was there typing on her computer, not even paying attention. She looked up just as her partner was sitting down.

"Hey, how's everything going?" she asked as she continued typing.

"Okay! The lieutenant would like to see you in his office ASAP. He sounds pissed too."

Cynthia stopped and looked at Theresa. She got up and headed toward his office. When she walked in, he slammed the door, causing everybody to look in that direction. Theresa already knew what was happening, but kept to herself.

"Are you that stupid or what? Your partner just came in here to tell me that you were seen by some little brat, fleeing a crime scene. He has proof that it was you, and she's ready to go to IA with it."

"I destroyed that video," she told him.

"You may have destroyed the video, but not the witness who can identify you. This is deeper than just you and me. If you go down, a lot of people might be going with you." He leaned back in his seat. "This is what I have to do until you take care of that problem. You are suspended, so I need your badge and gun. Make it look good too!"

She handed him her equipment and then stormed out the door. Theresa watched the whole thing unfold from her seat, enjoying the fact she had just ended a crooked cop's career. After Cynthia left, she decided to follow her, trying to collect more incriminating evidence on her. Instead of taking an unmarked car, she took her own.

"Soon you'll get what's coming to you," she mumbled to herself as she stayed a few cars behind so she wasn't spotted.

ELEVEN

"MOM, HAS AKIYLAH CALLED you? She told me she was going back to the islands to see her mom, but I just called to make sure she arrived safely, and they said she never came," Sahmeer said, looking worried.

"No, I haven't heard from her. Did you try calling her?"

"Several times," he stated matter of factly.

"Try her GPS. Her phone is in your name, so it's linked to yours."

Sahmeer smiled because it was something he should have thought of. When he tracked her through her GPS, it came back to a lodge in New York. He wondered what the hell she was doing out there. He

decided to take a trip to New York City. He called
Mike to see if he wanted to take a ride with him.

"What's up, bro?" Michael said, out of breath.

"Where you at right now?"

"I'm at one of my friend's cribs. Why? What's
up?"

"I thought you would want to take a trip out NY
with me and maybe catch a game at the Garden today," he said, hoping that Mike was down.

"Well, I'm going to be tied up all day, but if I can
free up some time, I'll hit you up."

Michael was literally tied up with Akiylah riding
his dick while Lorena sucked on her titties. She was
holding the phone to his ear as he talked.

"Okay, have fun with your jump-offs," Sahmeer
joked.

He ended the call and went into the bathroom to
take a quick shower. He was trying to find out why
his wife would lie about where she was going. All
types of thoughts were running through his head. He
had never cheated on his wife, so he hoped she
wasn't doing that to him.

After taking a shower, he got dressed and then had a drink of orange juice. Just as he was about to leave out, his cell phone rang. It was Akiylah!

"Where are you?" he snapped, not being able to control himself any longer. "I've texted and tried calling you a million times."

"Me in New York. Me was coming home early, but there's a holdover."

"Why didn't you call me and let me know something? You had me worried, Akiylah! As your husband, I'm entitled to know where my wife is and if she's okay."

"Me sorry, baby! Me will be home today sometime. Me love you," she smirked, trying to calm him down.

If only he could see what was going on behind her, he would file for a divorce immediately because of the transgressions of his wife. Michael was fucking Lorena doggy style across the chair, trying to get one last quickie in before they left.

"I love you too! See you when you get home," he said, and then ended the call.

He grabbed his car keys so he could make a few runs before Akiylah came home. As he headed out the door, Marcus was pulling up. Sahmeer decided that this was the time to settle any differences between the two.

"Hey, Dad, you got a minute?"

"What's up?" Marcus answered, closing the car door.

"I just wanted to say that no matter what, you are and forever will be my father. I love you more than anything in this world, besides Mom," he smirked causing them both to smile. "I just wanted to kill the elephant in the room and let you know that even if Uncle Kevin was still alive, he would continue to be just that."

"I appreciate that, buddy! I love you, man," Marcus said, hugging his son.

"There is something else," Sahmeer added. "I have decided to enter the draft this year, instead of waiting until next season. I think this would be the right thing to do for me. I don't want you and Mom to be mad or disappointed with me."

"We're never gonna be disappointed with you. That is actually a great idea, and I hope you get drafted so you can carry on our legacy. Do your mom know yet?"

"No!"

"How about we go tell her together before you head out. I'm sure she will be excited about it. She might even cook a big dinner for us tonight," he said smiling.

"You just want to eat! Come on, old man, let's do this."

"I got your old man." Marcus smiled.

They walked back into the house to deliver the news to his mom. She was more excited than he was. Marcus told him that he would find him an agent to start the transition. Everything seemed to be back to normal with their family.

***

Theresa had followed her partner to a gated community just outside of Philly, in the Broomall area. She watched as she and another female spoke briefly and then got into Cynthia's vehicle and pulled off. Theresa made sure that she stayed far enough back not to be seen, but close enough where she didn't lose sight of them. Thirty minutes later they pulled into an abandoned building, off of Parkside Avenue.

Theresa pulled behind a dumpster and hoped out, trying to sneak up behind them to see what they were up to. When she approached the window, she peeked inside and found them standing there talking. There was a third person in the room, but she couldn't see who it was. Needing a better view, she made her way around to the door. She was able to gain entrance, and crept through the building in search of the women.

"So what are we supposed to do with him? We just can't let him go now, or we really will be done. I don't understand why you didn't handle this yourself."

"Because it was your fuckup from the beginning that led us to this situation. If you would have done what I told you, we wouldn't be having this conversation," Cynthia pointed out in disbelief.

"My fuckup? Are you serious right now? I put my life on the line for this shit to work, and nobody else had enough courage to do what I was willing to do to make it happen."

"Ladies, ladies, please stop all this bickering, and let's focus on making this problem go away for good so we can all get back to our lives."

Theresa's eyes almost popped out of her head when she realized who was talking to them. She knew she had stumbled across a big scandal, but what?

"I agree. Let's take care of this problem so I can get back to work before anyone realizes I'm missing," Cynthia replied.

She walked over to a door and opened it up. What Theresa saw next made her heart drop. There was the kid that was helping them out with the case, badly beaten, sitting in a chair. Cynthia pulled him out to the middle of the floor and then smacked him twice, waking him up.

"Wake up, buddy!" She jerked his head back.

He opened his swollen eyes and looked at the three figures standing around him. You could tell that he was scared out of his mind. Cynthia pulled out her throwaway gun and aimed it at the kid's head. Theresa couldn't let this kid die like that. She removed her weapon from her side holster and then eased closer, with it aimed at her partner just in case.

"Would you hurry up so we can bury this snitch and get out of here?"

"Freeze, police!" Theresa yelled, causing everyone to look in her direction. "Drop the gun and keep your hands where I can see them. Cynthia, back away from that kid."

"And if I don't?"

"Then I will drop you where you stand. Now I won't ask again," Theresa said, showing no signs of backing down.

"Do what she said," Morgan stated. Cynthia tossed her gun toward Theresa's feet.

"Just calm down. There is more than enough of the pie to spread around," Cynthia said, raising her hands in the air.

"I don't want nothing to do with whatever you have going on. Now move over there, all of you," Theresa demanded.

They backed away from the kid and over toward the far end of the wall. Theresa kept her eyes on all of them as she reached into her pocket and pulled out her phone. She looked down to dial a number, and Cynthia took that moment as an opening and reached for her service pistol. She never got the chance to get a shot off. Theresa shot her twice, hitting her in the arm.

Boc! Boc!

Cynthia hit the ground holding her right arm. Theresa moved closer to the boy, reached into her back pocket, and removed her pocket knife. She cut the tape off of the kid and told him to get out of there. He stumbled out of the building, leaving her there with the three assailants.

"I know you," she said, looking at the other woman. "You're Michelle Green! Why would you kill your own husband?"

"Why don't you ask his cheating ass? Oh, my fault, you can't 'cause he's dead," Michelle shot back.

"Governor, what does this have to do with you? You are supposed to be a high-ranking official. Why get involved with these corrupt individuals?"

"There's a lot you don't know about me, and I don't have time to explain it either."

"Well I don't care if you explain it to me or not. Every one of you can explain it to a judge. Nobody else move if you don't want to get shot," Theresa stated, pressing send on her phone.

"We can pay you five million dollars! Me, Morgan, and Michelle can all give you a cut, and no one has to know about it," Cynthia replied.

"I don't want your money, Cynthia. All I want is to watch you and your friends rot in a cell as soon as my backup arrives."

"Drop the phone, officer. No one is coming to help you."

When she turned around, Pete was standing there with a gun pointed at her. She slowly let the phone drop to the floor.

"What are you doing, Pete?"

"The gun too!"

Just as she was about to lower the gun, the kid that was supposed to have left, hit Pete in the back with a pipe, causing him to stumble forward. That gave Theresa the opening she needed. She dove toward the ground, letting off two rounds in Pete's direction. One caught him in the leg as he dove out of the way.

Theresa grabbed the kid's hand, and they ran behind a wall, trying to get out of the way of gunfire. She immediately returned fire to keep them at bay until help arrived. During the whole ordeal, she never disconnected the call. She just hoped help was on the way.

"Drop your weapons and give up. Help is on the way!"

"We all know that they're not, so if you come out now, I'll make your death quick," Pete said, letting off a couple of rounds in her direction.

"Come on, we need to find a way out of here. If we stay here, we're sitting ducks," she told the boy, looking around for an exit.

Michelle helped Cynthia up, while Morgan and Pete went after Theresa and the boy. When they didn't hear anything, they charged around the corner, but no one was there.

"In there," Morgan whispered, pointing to the room ahead of them.

They approached with caution, making sure it wasn't a setup. Pete kicked the door in and was met with a bullet to the chest. He fell backward, dying before he hit the ground. Morgan started firing into the room wildly.

"Stay down," Theresa whispered creeping around the back of the room.

Morgan walked real slow looking for any sign of movement. The boy stuck his head up trying to be nosey and was spotted. By the time he ducked back down, Morgan was on him. He pointed the gun at the kid.

"You should have kept your mouth shut," he said, aiming the gun at the kid.

Boc! Boc! Boc! Boc!

Morgan fell forward, landing on his face in front of the boy. He closed his eyes as blood from the wounds splashed on his clothes and face. Theresa stood behind him with smoke still coming from her gun.

"Let's go," she said.

As they made their way to the exit, a bunch of men dressed in all black came rushing in. They were carrying assault weapons and shields.

"Drop your weapon and get down on the ground," one of them shouted.

"I'm a cop," Theresa yelled, dropping her gun.

They quickly grabbed her and the boy and then escorted them outside. When they stepped out, there were cops everywhere. She looked over and saw that they had Cynthia and Michelle in custody. Her lieutenant walked over to her, put his arm on her shoulders, and then gave her a hug.

"Are y'all okay?" he asked.

"Yes, but how did you know?"

"You left your phone on when you dialed 911, and dispatch recorded everything that was being said, at the same time tracking your location. When we heard, you mention their names, that is what helped us identify who was who. That was good police work, Detective. If you hadn't done that, she probably would have gotten away. If there's one thing I hate, it's dirty politicians and cops.

"I second that," Theresa smiled.

"Go home and get some rest. We'll debrief you first thing in the morning."

Theresa went home and took a hot shower and then enjoyed the rest of the night with her family. The next day she was debriefed, and the kid she saved was placed in protective custody until he testified at trial. Michelle took a deal in exchange for her testimony against Cynthia and everyone that had something to do with it.

***

Two Months Later

"Hurry up, Akiylah. We have to leave now if we want to be on time for the draft," Sahmeer yelled out to her.

"Me coming now," she replied, walking out of the bathroom. She was rocking a black strapless dress with six-inch stilettos. She had her hair down, showing off how long it was.

Sahmeer had to admire how beautiful his wife looked. They rushed out of the hotel room, trying to get to Madison Square Garden, where the draft was being held. Sahmeer was scheduled to go in the top five, and he was hoping to join Carmelo Anthony with the Knicks. Since they were only a couple of blocks away, they decided to walk. They took a shortcut through a pathway to make up some time.

"Hold up," Akiylah said, stopping to remove her stilettos.

Sahmeer stopped to wait for her and never saw the masked man coming up from behind him until it was too late. He stabbed Sahmeer twice in the neck. Sahmeer tried to scream, but no words came out.

When he reached for the man's mask and pulled it off, Michael smiled at him.

"Sorry, bro, she's mines!"

"Text Good2Go at 31996 to receive new release updates via text message.

BOOKS BY GOOD2GO AUTHORS

SILK WHITE — **SILK WHITE** — **JACOB SPEARS** — **JACOB SPEARS** — **SILK WHITE**

ERNEST MORRIS — **ERNEST MORRIS** — **MYCHEA** — **MYCHEA** — **MYCHEA**

MYCHEA — **MYCHEA** — **ERNEST MORRIS** — **SILK WHITE** — **ASIA HILL**

ASIA HILL — **MYCHEA** — **MYCHEA** — **SILK WHITE** — **SILKWHITE**

SLUMPED PART 1
JASON BRENT

SILK WHITE
STRANDED

TEARS OF A HUSTLER

TEARS OF A HUSTLER 2
SILK WHITE

TEARS OF A HUSTLER 3
SILK WHITE

TEARS OF A HUSTLER
YOU'VE BEEN WARNED
SILK WHITE

SILK WHITE
TEARS OF A HUSTLER 5
THE SPADES

SILK WHITE
TEARS OF A HUSTLER 6

THE TEFLON QUEEN
SILK WHITE

THE TEFLON QUEEN 2
SILK WHITE

THE TEFLON QUEEN 3
HARD TO KILL
SILK WHITE

THE TEFLON QUEEN 4
SILK WHITE

THE TEFLON QUEEN 5
SILK WHITE

THE TEFLON QUEEN
NO MERCY
SILK WHITE

THE PANTY RIPPER
REALITY WAY

THE PANTY RIPPER
REALITY WAY

TIED TO A BOSS
J.L. ROSE

TIME IS MONEY
SILK WHITE

YOUNG GOONZ
REALITY WAY

To order books, please fill out the order form below:
*To order films please go to **www.good2gofilms.com***

Name:_____

Address:_____

City: _____ State: _____ Zip Code: _____

Phone:_____

Email:_____

Method of Payment: Check   VISA   MASTERCARD

Credit Card#:_____

Name as it appears on card: _____

Signature: _____

Item Name	Price	Qty	Amount
48 Hours to Die – Silk White	$14.99		
A Hustler's Dream - Ernest Morris	$14.99		
A Hustler's Dream 2 - Ernest Morris	$14.99		
Bloody Mayhem Down South	$14.99		
Business Is Business – Silk White	$14.99		
Business Is Business 2 – Silk White	$14.99		
Business Is Business 3 – Silk White	$14.99		
Childhood Sweethearts – Jacob Spears	$14.99		
Childhood Sweethearts 2 – Jacob Spears	$14.99		
Childhood Sweethearts 3 - Jacob Spears	$14.99		
Childhood Sweethearts 4 - Jacob Spears	$14.99		
Flipping Numbers – Ernest Morris	$14.99		
Flipping Numbers 2 – Ernest Morris	$14.99		
He Loves Me, He Loves You Not - Mychea	$14.99		
He Loves Me, He Loves You Not 2 - Mychea	$14.99		
He Loves Me, He Loves You Not 3 - Mychea	$14.99		
He Loves Me, He Loves You Not 4 – Mychea	$14.99		
He Loves Me, He Loves You Not 5 – Mychea	$14.99		
Lord of My Land – Jay Morrison	$14.99		
Lost and Turned Out – Ernest Morris	$14.99		
Married To Da Streets – Silk White	$14.99		
M.E.R.C. - Make Every Rep Count Health and Fitness	$14.99		
My Besties – Asia Hill	$14.99		
My Besties 2 – Asia Hill	$14.99		
My Besties 3 – Asia Hill	$14.99		
My Besties 4 – Asia Hill	$14.99		
My Boyfriend's Wife - Mychea	$14.99		
My Boyfriend's Wife 2 – Mychea	$14.99		
Naughty Housewives – Ernest Morris	$14.99		
Naughty Housewives 2 – Ernest Morris	$14.99		

Naughty Housewives 3 – Ernest Morris	$14.99		
Naughty Housewives 4 – Ernest Morris	$14.99		
Never Be The Same – Silk White	$14.99		
Stranded – Silk White	$14.99		
Slumped – Jason Brent	$14.99		
Tears of a Hustler - Silk White	$14.99		
Tears of a Hustler 2 - Silk White	$14.99		
Tears of a Hustler 3 - Silk White	$14.99		
Tears of a Hustler 4- Silk White	$14.99		
Tears of a Hustler 5 – Silk White	$14.99		
Tears of a Hustler 6 – Silk White	$14.99		
The Panty Ripper - Reality Way	$14.99		
The Panty Ripper 3 – Reality Way	$14.99		
The Solution – Jay Morrison	$14.99		
The Teflon Queen – Silk White	$14.99		
The Teflon Queen 2 – Silk White	$14.99		
The Teflon Queen 3 – Silk White	$14.99		
The Teflon Queen 4 – Silk White	$14.99		
The Teflon Queen 5 – Silk White	$14.99		
The Teflon Queen 6 - Silk White	$14.99		
The Vacation – Silk White	$14.99		
Tied To A Boss - J.L. Rose	$14.99		
Tied To A Boss 2 - J.L. Rose	$14.99		
Tied To A Boss 3 - J.L. Rose	$14.99		
Tied To A Boss 4 - J.L. Rose	$14.99		
Time Is Money - Silk White	$14.99		
Two Mask One Heart – Jacob Spears and Trayvon Jackson	$14.99		
Two Mask One Heart 2 – Jacob Spears and Trayvon Jackson	$14.99		
Two Mask One Heart 3 – Jacob Spears and Trayvon Jackson	$14.99		
Young Goonz – Reality Way	$14.99		
Young Legend – J.L. Rose	$14.99		
Subtotal:			
Tax:			
Shipping (Free) U.S. Media Mail:			
Total:			

Make Checks Payable To:
Good2Go Publishing
7311 W Glass Lane,
Laveen, AZ 85339

CPSIA information can be obtained
at www.ICGtesting.com
Printed in the USA
LVOW13s1605140417
530892LV00008B/423/P